"Get out of here, Hannah Randall,"

Sam muttered, holding her tight to him.

Startled out of the spell his touch had woven around her, Hannah said, confused, "What do you mean?"

"I'm like that old king, the one who turned anything he touched into gold. He killed everything, everything he loved. I'm a destroyer, Hannah Randall. I destroy everything I touch." His words ripped into the room.

Suddenly, his lips took hers, hungry and despairing and pulling her down into a world dark with yearning she'd never known existed, where skin pulsed and hummed, and his mouth bound her with chains she'd never dreamed could be forged in a fire of touching and wanting.

"Run, Hannah," he said in a barely heard voice. "While you can. Run before I destroy you, too."

Dear Reader,

It's March—and spring is just around the corner. We all know spring is the season of love, but at Silhouette Romance, every season is romantic, and every month we offer six heartwarming stories that capture the laughter, the tears, the sheer joy of falling in love. This month is no exception!

Honey, I'm Home by Rena McKay is a delightful reminder that even the most dashing hero is a little boy at heart, and Lindsay Longford's *Pete's Dragon* will reaffirm your belief in the healing power of love...and make-believe. The intense passion of Suzanne Carey's *Navajo Wedding* will keep you spellbound, the sizzling *Two To Tango* by Kristina Logan will quite simply make you want to dance, and Linda Varner's *As Sweet as Candy* will utterly charm you.

No month is complete without our special WRITTEN IN THE STARS selection. This month we have the exciting, challenging Pisces man in Anne Peters's *Storky Jones Is Back in Town*.

Throughout the year we'll be publishing stories of love by all your favorite Silhouette Romance authors—Diana Palmer, Suzanne Carey, Annette Broadrick, Brittany Young and many, many more. The Silhouette Romance authors and editors love to hear from readers, and we'd love to hear from *you!*

Happy Reading!

Valerie Susan Hayward
Senior Editor

LINDSAY LONGFORD

Pete's Dragon

Silhouette *Romance*

Published by Silhouette Books New York

America's Publisher of Contemporary Romance

To my aunt, Pearl Moon, for opening her home and making room.
To my mother-in-law, Alice Morel, who taught my son what good cooking is.

ACKNOWLEDGMENTS

With grateful appreciation and many thanks to John Hare, director of the South
Florida Museum/Bishop Planetarium, Bradenton, Florida, for gracious
permission to mention the museum and Snooty, a rare and wondrous manatee,
and to Jennifer Hamilton of the museum for her generous contribution of
information. May Snooty and the other twelve hundred manatees in Florida live
long and prosper in spite of man's encroachment.

Special thanks to Colin Flecken of Naperville Jeep Eagle, Inc., Naperville,
Illinois, for the time he took to share such wonderful stories and information
about the origins of the Jeep and to help work out technical points.

SILHOUETTE BOOKS
300 E. 42nd St., New York, N.Y. 10017

PETE'S DRAGON

ISBN: 0-373-08854-X

First Silhouette Books printing March 1992

Printed in the U.S.A.

Books by Lindsay Longford

Silhouette Romance

Jake's Child #696
Pete's Dragon #854

Silhouette Intimate Moments

Cade Boudreau's Revenge #390

LINDSAY LONGFORD,

like most writers, is a reader. She even reads tooth-paste labels in desperation! A former high school English teacher with an M.A. in literature, she began writing romances because she wanted to create stories that touched readers' emotions by transporting them to a world where good things happened to good people and happily ever after is possible with a little work.

Her first book, *Jake's Child,* was nominated for Best New Series Author, Best Silhouette Romance and received a Special Achievement Award for Best First Series Book from *Romantic Times*. It was also a finalist in the Romance Writers of America RITA contest for Best First Book.

Pete's
Dragon

Chapter One

Every evening at twilight, the dragon came to the garden.

Fireflies darted through the long, seed-heavy grass, weaving patterns of flickering yellow in the waiting silence, and stalks of tall sunflowers stood sentinel in the deep shadows of one corner near the slats of the unpainted wooden fence.

Petey heard the sputter and roar of a motorcycle down the road, but once more all around him like a cloak, silence fell, thick and heavy.

Framed in windows, people moved unheard in and out of light and darkness in mysterious pantomimes of family rituals. Dishes clinked against each other in these rooms, and mothers and fathers said wondrous things to children gathered at the tables.

Petey scratched the mosquito bite on his bare leg as he waited and watched the silent, moving pictures.

A hush came over the garden.

Then the earth inhaled and the tall grass bent forward, making invisible footsteps in the summer night.

And Petey heard the rustling of leathery wings and the hissing approach of the dragon.

There was a metallic clanking and creaking of scales.

Through the morning-glory vines thick on the wooden fence, Petey glimpsed the glowing red eye that lifted in the dark and finally turned in his direction. He heard the hissing whistle that came low and eerily to his straining ears in the almost darkness.

Smoky breath drifted to him on the evening breeze.

He sucked in his breath and rubbed the shivers on his arms.

The dragon had come!

Petey wiggled his fingers through the vines and made the peephole bigger. Pressing his eye to the fence, he saw the dark bulk of the dragon settling on the grass under the moss-draped shadows of the oak tree. As the dragon hunched there, its red eye burned and glittered.

"Hey," Petey whispered. "Hey," he whispered again, more loudly, shivering with excitement. He stuck his thumb in his mouth.

On each of the three nights since he and his mom had moved into this house, Petey had watched for the dragon.

From his upstairs bedroom the first night, Petey had looked out the window down onto the yard next door and had seen the stately approach of the dragon, smelled its smoke borne upward to him in the summer night and watched from his windowsill until the dragon's red eye finally dimmed with sleep and closed.

The next morning Petey had leapt out of bed and raced out to the hole in the fence separating the two yards. Shoving the vines aside, he saw only the strange, smooth imprints that marked the track of the dragon, the drag of its tail.

All day long, Petey hovered near the fence, waiting.

All day long, the shades of the house next door were drawn, the hum of a window air-conditioner the only sound, until shadows stretched long and black in the garden and fireflies sparkled in the dark.

Each night in those quiet moments poised between dusk and dark, while Petey's mother washed the dishes and Petey watched with quivering hopefulness and gathered his courage to speak, the dragon came to the garden.

Tonight was the third night.

"Hey, there," Petey finally said again as loudly as he could in his best Sunday-school voice, adding for politeness and not knowing how else to address a dragon, "Sir."

The fierce eye turned to him, its angry glow sending Petey tumbling from the sawed-off tree trunk where he'd perched.

"Who's there?" hissed the dragon. His voice was deep and whistling.

"Jes' me," Petey said through his quivering lips as he climbed back up and peeked into the dragon's yard.

"Go away, Just Me," the dragon growled amid a flurry of fire sparks and smoke.

"Where to?" Petey wondered, worried. Dragons had awful powers. He'd sooner stay home, but if the dragon wanted him to go somewhere, well, Petey didn't think he'd have any say-so about it, dragons being pretty much hard to argue with.

"Anywhere. I don't care. Away from here." The rumble and hiss filled the air.

Petey let out a whoosh of relief. He hadn't wanted to go very far from his mom. "Okay, I'm jes' anywhere here in my yard. Under the sunflowers," Petey offered. "You wanna talk?"

"No." The dragon's voice was irritable and pain filled.

Petey hadn't thought the dragon wanted to talk, but his mom always said you had to carry on conversation when you met somebody, it was good manners, and anyway, meeting a dragon seemed like just about the best time to have a conversation.

Wondering what would cause a dragon pain and struck by the memory of the hot dogs he'd eaten at the Fourth of July picnic right before they moved, Petey asked, "You got a pain in your belly?"

There was a long silence. Finally the dragon muttered in a low voice, "No."

"I had a bad bellyache once and throwed up all over my daddy." Petey thought about the purple grape juice and hot dogs that had splooshed out. "He was mad. *Very.*" Petey stuck his thumb in his mouth again before adding, "Tha's why he 'vorced me, I expect."

He squashed one of the leaves on the vine and went on, not really sure why he was telling the dragon all this. Mommy always said family business was private, but the dragon wouldn't talk, and somebody had to hold up that conversation thing his mom was always reminding him about. "Mommy says daddies 'vorce mommies, not their boys, but she don't know about me throwing up all that stuff on Daddy's new coat, so I expect she's wrong." Petey sighed.

The dragon's hissing sigh echoed Petey's.

"I expect Daddy was just tired of both of us. We were awful noisy. And I made lots of messes. Daddy said I made more messes than there was stars in the sky." Petey looked up at the stars. "That's a lot of messes." He rubbed his eyes. "Prob'ly a jillion zillion or somethin'.''

Petey watched the firefly that had landed right in front of his nose.

Maybe he could catch one and keep it in his room. He'd like having the small glow all night, and he didn't like thinking about THE VORCE. That was how his daddy talked. In all those BIG LETTERS. THE VORCE, HANNAH, I WANT THE VORCE AND SOON, HANNAH. That's what his daddy kept saying over and over until Petey covered up his ears.

Petey told the dragon about the big letters, carefully making sure that the dragon knew it had been his, Petey's fault.

The dragon's eye glowed dully, and his ferocious voice sounded tired. "Go home, little boy, I'm tired."

Petey yawned. "*Not* a little boy. I'm Petey Robert Randall. I've been a *big* boy a long time."

"I see," hissed the dragon in a fading rumble, and resettled himself with a clanking and creaking. There was a long silence before the dragon continued in a tone filled with reluctance. "How big are you?"

"*Very* big. I don't weared diapers for a *very* long time and I go the bathroom all by myself but not at the mall, and I don't wet my bed at night anymore. But I did last night," Petey added, wanting to be honest.

"I see," growled the dragon again as he laid his head on the dark grass, his red eye only a faint glow. "Terrific, I'm really happy for you, but I meant, how old?"

Petey counted out silently on his fingers. "Prob'ly almost five. I will go to kindergarten when school starts. But I don't want to."

A drawn-out hiss in the dark, and then the dragon said, "Go home, Petey Robert Randall. Please."

Petey wished he could see how long the dragon's tail was. "Don't want to go home." He scratched his leg again. Prob'ly he had chiggers from the moss. Mommy was always telling him not to wrap moss around his legs, but he liked how hairy they looked all covered in moss, like the black, thick hair on his daddy's legs. He scratched again. "Want to talk with you," he insisted.

Suddenly the dragon's voice was angry, filled with sharpness that seemed to glitter in the air. "Go home now, Petey Robert Randall! I don't want you here!"

There was a terrifying rattling and banging that sent Petey scooting down to the bottom of the fence and heading for home before he remembered his manners. Running back as fast as he could with his heart pounding, he skidded to a halt and yelled through the knothole, "Bye. Nicemeetingyouseeyouagain! Sir!"

Not even looking over his shoulder, he pelted to the open back door of his house. No telling what the dragon would do, but they could do anything, and he sure didn't want his dragon mad at him.

Inside the sweltering kitchen, Hannah lifted her hands out of the soapy dishwater and looked up at the sound of her son's voice. "Petey?" she called out through the screen door, and waited. She brushed her damp hair back from her face. It was so hot this time of year. She'd forgotten Florida summer nights were this smotheringly hot and damp. Mildew had already formed on the shoes she'd unpacked and put into the small bedroom closet.

Not wanting to let in the mosquitoes, she kept her hand on the latch, ready to let her perpetual-motion machine barrel into the house.

Out of the dark he raced to her, his left foot flipping inward. Head down and full tilt, stumbling when he landed wrong on his left leg. He was so small and fragile. She worried all the time about how she was going to protect him. What if something happened to her? What then? Hannah wiped her suddenly damp palms down her faded shorts and reminded herself not to think about the future. One day at a time. She could cope with that. One day.

She opened the door, her throat closing tightly against the fears that came crowding up from inside.

"Hey, sugar," she said, wrapping her arms tightly around him and sniffing his special little-boy smell. Petey. Blinded and in a roomful of people, she'd know him. Sometimes she'd walk into his bedroom and breathe in the essence of her son and be comforted.

Petey squirmed. "You're squishing me, Mommy."

Hannah loosened her grip. "Sorry, honey buns. There—" she picked a twig out of his hair "—better?"

"Yep." He butted his head against her. "Guess what?"

"What?" She had to watch this new tendency to cling. Petey needed security and routine, not an anxious mother bedeviled by fears. Tugging at his ear, she smiled down at his square face. "Those nasty old mosquitoes been eating you alive? Look there, you're covered with bites."

He scratched hard.

Hannah tousled his hair and gently urged him to the bathroom. "Let's put something on those, or you're going to itch all night long, sugar."

"Not the mosquitoes, Mommy, that's not what to guess. Somethin' big." He stretched his arms as wide as they could reach. "Somethin' next door. In the garden!"

"A dog?" Pulling the string on the circular fluorescent fixture, Hannah blinked. This bathroom needed the softening light of an incandescent bulb, as well as new wallpaper, she thought ruefully, opening the white metal cabinet and taking out a can of spray ointment. She lifted up the door and forced the bent hinges into alignment so it would shut. At least the place was clean, she consoled herself, shaking the can. Run-down, but clean.

"Bigger'n a dog, for sure!" His eyes were round and shining.

"An elephant?" She'd played this game before and she knew Petey's rules.

"Not a lelephunt. Bigger!" He thought for a second. "Prob'ly."

"Hold out your legs, sugar. Let's get those taken care of first, okay?"

Petey nodded. "You got one more guess!" He wiggled and stuck his legs out.

"Well, let me think. Bigger than an elephant, hmm?"

His hair flopped into his eyes with his vigorous nod.

Hannah sprayed the anesthetic up the front and back of his sturdy brown legs, wincing at the red lumps that covered him. He'd sneaked out of the kitchen before she could put mosquito repellent on him. "We'll have to spray you down after your bath again, Petey, but at least you won't be scratching between now and then." If he kept scratching the way he was, the bites would get infected, but she didn't tell him that. Better to spray an extra time.

His thumb was in his mouth again.

She couldn't say anything. He'd just started sucking his thumb in the past few weeks. One more problem to cope with. But not tonight. If Petey found solace in the small action, that was good enough for her these days. "I give up, sugar, what's in the garden?"

"A dragon!"

Hannah smiled. "Silly me. I should have guessed. Of course. I think a dragon would maybe be bigger than an elephant. Unless it was a baby dragon?"

Petey looked away. Animation drained out of him.

The light fixture sputtered as she sprayed his arms. His thumb went right back into his mouth when she'd finished that arm, and he sat slumped on the toilet while she anointed the back of his neck. Finally she sighed. She'd messed up the rules without knowing it. "Why so quiet, honey?"

His big brown eyes stared up at her from under his silky eyebrows. Slowly and uncertainly he took his thumb out of his mouth and said very carefully, watching her the whole time, "Been talking with my dragon, Mommy." He waited, a strangely grown-up look in his brown eyes.

Hannah sighed and smoothed his eyebrows. She knew her usually sunny-natured son was lonely and sad these days, but she could handle the thumb sucking better than she could this new obsession with his make-believe friends. "Oh, Petey, honey, I wish you'd—"

She stopped. Maybe Petey needed an imaginary friend. Lord knew she was only a step away from talking to the walls herself.

"You don't b'lieve me." His deep voice accused her. A pint-size prosecutor in khaki shorts that had seen better days a long time ago, he fixed her with that unblinking stare.

"Oh, honey." Hannah stumbled over the words. What was the best way to handle this business? Was it typical behavior, or did it come from his insecurities over the divorce, one more fault to be laid at her door? "Petey, you know, don't you? Of course you do. Dragons aren't real, honey. They're just in books."

"I know." He stuck his thumb in his mouth again. "But *my* dragon is real. And he talked to me," Petey added stubbornly, glaring at her. "You should b'lieve me." His face was all outraged innocence. "Petey Robert Randall don't lie."

Hannah gave up. "I know, honey." She tapped his nose. "You've always been my good boy."

What difference did it make if Petey needed to talk to dragons? Who did it hurt? Fiercely she hugged her son, aching to make the world beautiful and shining for him, wanting to give him the moon and stars and not able to give him anything except herself.

"You're squishing me again, Mommy." He wiggled loose.

"So I am." She riffled her fingers through his sticky hair. Heaven only knew what he'd gotten into.

"You gotta quit squishing me so much. I'm not a baby no more."

"Of course you're not. You're my designated packer-up guy. Babies are lousy at packing stuff up. What would I want with a baby, anyway, for goodness' sake?" She gently poked his chin. "So, big-guy Petey Robert Randall, what did you and your dragon talk about?" Hannah sat on the toilet lid and lifted her grubby son into her lap, cuddling him against her. "About knights and ladies and battles?"

"No, Mommy, I *told* you. My dragon's *real*. We talked about nowaday things, not olden days."

"Oh," Hannah said, nonplussed. "I see. Um, what's your dragon's name?"

"Don't know." Petey yawned. "You always say asking personal stuff is rude. Didn't ask. He's a cranky dragon."

"Oh," Hannah repeated. Bracing her toes on the cast-iron tub with its ball and clawed feet—maybe where Petey had gotten the idea of dragons?—Hannah rocked her son. "I guess dragons have bad days, too, huh?"

"I guess," said Petey with another yawn.

"How'd you like to have to burp fire all the time?" If Petey needed an imaginary world, by heaven, the least she could do was live in it with him. "I think it would give me a stomach ache."

"Nope. Asked him if his belly hurt. He said it didn't."

She laughed. "Well, that was considerate of you, honey. Wonder what a dragon would take for a tummyache, anyway?"

"A box of saltines." Petey nestled his head into the curve of Hannah's shoulder.

Hannah felt his warm breath on her arm. He was all she had. All she wanted. "Well, I don't know about dragons, but I do know about boys, and I think I have a boy who needs to go to bed."

"Too early," Petey said around the yawn stretching his mouth, and squirreled his hot little face into her damp neck.

She'd have to get a fan for his room. That would come first.

"I not ready to go to sleep right now."

His yawn tickled her chin.

"I'm sure you're right, but by the time we finish your bath and story, don't you think just maybe you might be sleepy?" Hannah teased, knowing his head would hit the pillow and he'd be asleep before she could walk out the bedroom door. "C'mon, sugar, let's scrub some of this glop off you and see if there really is a big boy underneath here."

Gently she stood him on the floor and lifted the bottom of his shirt.

"I can do it," he insisted, jerking his shirt up and tangling himself in the neckline.

"Of course you can." Hannah swallowed the lump in her throat. He was growing up so fast. And the world was full of sharp edges for little boys to run into. "How'd you like to have your story out on the back porch tonight? It'll be cooler. Do you want milk and cookies? Or lemonade since it's so hot?"

"Memonade," he said, stretching his arms up for her to lift him into the oversize tub, "two stories from my book and a mommy story."

"You bet, sugarplum."

Swinging him into the water, Hannah tried not to think of the hours of work still left to do. Unpacked boxes. Paperwork still to be done. Bills that had to be juggled, some to be paid, some to wait. The job interview. Soaping up the rag and swooping it over his face, she smiled at her son, who was busily poking his finger into his belly button. "F'ree stories. All about magic and happy endings."

And when she carried her soap-sweet boy out to the dark, screened-in back porch, Hannah sat in the metal rocker and read to Petey about talking crocodiles and gentle giants while she tried not to think about the ungentle days that lay before them, tried not to cry with exhaustion and fear.

In a rhythmic undertone, the squeaking runners punctuated the story-telling while overhead the southern constellations shone in the deep soft night, black as only country southern nights can be.

"Lub dub," said Petey after a long while, moving his cheek against her left breast.

"What's that, sugar?"

"Lub dub, lub dub. That's the beat of your heart," he said sleepily. "You smell good, Mommy."

"So do you, sugar," Hannah whispered, and squished him tightly to her, rocking on in the darkness until she heard his tiny bubbling snores.

On the other side of the fence, in the dark garden, Sam listened to Hannah's husky voice. Its music, low and inescapable, held him there. Held him in spite of his fingers clenched on the chair, held him in spite of the pain. This pain was different, and he wasn't prepared for it. A pain deep, deep inside, in the hollow blackness of himself.

Since the woman, Hannah—he knew her name now—and her son had moved in, their daily bustle had intruded on his isolation. He'd ignored them for the most part. Hadn't wanted to see the woman's pale-faced exhaustion, the buzz-saw cheerfulness of her son as they unloaded the white hatchback that held their belongings.

But, in spite of himself, he found his eyes wandering in the direction of the house next to his. Sitting in the empty darkness of his yard that first night, he'd seen her, Hannah, spotlighted in her uncurtained kitchen window, slumped over the rickety table, her shoulders shaking with silent sobs.

Unable to look away, Sam had watched as her head turned and the small boy crawled up into her lap. There had been something about the way her hand cradled his head, the tenderness in her head bent to the boy that had been unbearable to watch.

A long swath of her streaky brown hair had curled forward over her shoulder, and the child, rubbing his eyes with one hand, had tangled his chubby fist into the light brown coil near his face.

The woman had smiled with a look of melting tenderness and kissed the small hand twisting in her long hair and rested her cheek against the boy's fist.

Remembering the look on her face, Sam fought off the black wings of despair folding around him. No reason to fight, easier to surrender to the darkness.

No surrender. Surviving was his punishment. Pain, his penance. He didn't have the right to give up.

Slowly, finger by finger, he unclenched his hand.

Once more her voice stilled his movements. "Hush, little baby, don't you cry, Momma's gonna sing you a lullaby."

Bluesy and sweet, like an alto sax, her voice lingered over the words of the old nursery rhyme and hung in the hot darkness.

"You'll still be the sweetest boy in town...." The last notes trembled in the still air, falling around him like a blessing until they faded.

Sam ground the heel of his hand into his dry, aching eyes. He should never have let Arnie talk him into spending the summer here. A bad mistake. Arnie had caught him on the darkest of many dark days, when making even the smallest decision had been beyond him. Arnie had just bulled in and done everything. A friend.

A rocker squeaked. "Shh, sugar, I'm just going to carry you up to bed now. You go back to sleep, hear?" Her shoulders and head appeared above the top of the fence. Her hair was sliding down from its haphazard topknot.

She was small. Even standing on her raised porch, she was barely visible to him. The porch door banged behind her, and she moved into the kitchen, coming more fully into view as she paused at the metal sink and turned the spigot on.

Her son's left foot was caught in the side pocket of her faded green shorts. His other leg dangled around her hips.

Her hips were round and soft. Sam shut his eyes.

When he opened them, she'd balanced her son on one hip while she held the glass to him. Her pale legs gleamed in the light and then disappeared as she walked quickly out of the room, pulling the light chain as she left.

The afterimage glowed in his eyes like a half-forgotten dream and then it, too, winked out, leaving him alone and in darkness.

Hannah tucked the sheet under the mattress. Petey liked to be covered up, even on the hottest nights. Safety, security, who knew why, a new habit like the thumb sucking. She straightened, rubbing the dull ache in her back.

"Mommy?"

"Hmm?" She stroked the back of her hand against the soft, soft skin of his face. "What is it, sugar?"

"My dragon's real, you know." Petey curled a small bilious green dinosaur under his chin.

"Oh, honey." Hannah looked out the window at the dark house next to hers. On higher ground and raised up on stilts because of the building codes designed to prevent flooding here on the Gulf Coast, the house towered over her old two-story and was more typical of the neighborhood than the seediness of her rented house. "I think that house is empty, sugar. The yard's all shaggy, and I haven't seen anybody since we moved in."

"He's not anybody. He's a dragon. And you could see him if you looked."

Hannah swallowed her groan. "All right. I'll look, okay? Tomorrow."

Petey drew his thick eyebrows together. "You promise?"

"I promise." Hannah kissed him. "Go to sleep, sugar. It's late."

Once again Hannah looked over at the house that overshadowed hers. Its brooding darkness and overgrown garden made her uneasy. Fancifully she thought it looked as though it were holding its breath, waiting for something, held in the grip of some dark enchantment.

She'd been telling Petey too many stories.

Hannah left Petey's door open. They both liked the lights on at night these days.

In the kitchen she opened up the small refrigerator and took out a toy-sized metal tray, popping the ice cubes into a glass and pouring iced tea over them. Sipping, she tried to focus her thoughts, keep them controlled and not let them go skittering off like mice turned loose in a cheese factory.

Through the arch leading to what the Realtor had euphemistically called the "dining" room, she contemplated the stacks of boxes leaning against the walls. Well, wishing and a quarter would get her only a cup of coffee. No, not even a cup of coffee these days.

Twenty-seven years old and starting all over. Not quite. She had Petey. He was worth everything. She had Petey. That made her life worth something. Made *her* worth something, no matter what vicious words Carl had thrown at her. Petey.

Sighing, she walked into her dining room. Maybe she could get some of the confounded boxes emptied before morning. At least she'd be cooler working now.

Hannah raised the window all the way up and then opened the door of the screened porch. Maybe there would be a cross breeze.

Standing at the door and looking out at the dark garden next door, she thought she caught a faint hint of smoke. Tobacco? She sniffed. It was gone, but for a fleeting moment, breathing it in, she'd felt less alone. Somewhere out there in the night and silence, someone else couldn't sleep.

Petey's dragon? Hannah laughed and stretched, lightness moving through her for the first day in months. She untied the bottom three buttons of her shirt and fanned the tails out, letting the air dry the perspiration that slid down her back. People *had* survived in Florida without air-conditioning, hadn't they?

In the meantime, music and work would help. She flipped on the radio dial and turned the music low with one hand and dragged the first box to her with the other.

There were a lot worse things than being awake and alone in the late night. With music filling the corners of the room and the vagrant breeze teasing the damp hair at her neck, Hannah felt peace steal into her, blunting her frantic, fidgety thoughts. Slicing open a box and lifting out wadded newspaper, she decided that maybe, just maybe, things would look a whole lot brighter tomorrow.

Lingering in the garden, Sam let the low notes of the music eddy out to him. He'd seen the gleam of her smooth skin as she untied her shirt. The glimpses of her through the open window, the lingering notes of the music wove a spell around him, chained him where he sat and blessedly kept his demons at bay.

He knew he should go in, not stay in the darkness watching like a hungry child at the window of a candy store. But he couldn't make himself leave. The music on the radio, the distant sound of her voice singing with the late-night music held him captive in his garden as she worked.

Hannah winced as she opened her eyes in the hot, red glare of the morning sun that burned ruthlessly into her uncurtained bedroom, and decided that, yes indeedy, things certainly looked brighter. Groaning, she shut her eyes against that fierce brightness. Her feet hit the floor with a thud, but the rest of her body rebelled, staying firmly horizontal.

When had she gone to bed? Had she changed her clothes? Pulling one eyelid open, she glanced down. She hadn't. Well, wonderful.

Lying there, Hannah let the sun burn down on her. A garbage truck banged down the street, cans clanking and rolling.

Her appointment. She had a job appointment at nine! Shower! Petey! Breakfast. Hannah stood straight up, glancing wildly at the blinking green numbers. Eight o'clock. She'd never make it. Maybe. Never. She had to.

Of course Petey dawdled. Of course the first egg she cracked open for his breakfast hit the floor.

And of course her car chose to assert itself and refuse to start. It was personal, Hannah thought, breathing deeply and rubbing the steering wheel. Very personal. Her car always started. She was the one who'd always taken it for checkups, not Carl. She was the one who made sure its oil was changed regularly, not Carl. Never Carl. He didn't have time for things like the car. Or her. Or Petey.

Frustrated and near tears, she banged the wheel with her forehead. Definitely personal. Ungrateful car.

"Mommy? Why aren't we going? Mommy, please, don't cry."

From the safety of his bedroom, Sam watched the blades of the ceiling fan circle slowly, its motor a mind-deadening hum, yet he still heard the boy's woeful sobs. Not his problem. He let his eyes follow the intricate lines of the spider web in the far corner of the room. He frowned, remembering the anxiety in the boy's voice.

Pulling himself up and out of bed with the bar on the wall, Sam lifted the lower edge of the window shade. His bedroom was at the front of the house, and he looked straight down into her car at her determined, anxious face.

Not his problem. Not going to be his problem.

Nothing he could do. He couldn't fix her car. Not anymore.

Sam dropped the shade and lay back down. The blades circled smoothly over his head, and the breeze they generated rattled the edges of the blinds against the partially open window. Click, click, click. Restful. Quiet.

Pulling himself up again, Sam looked out the window. Didn't her hair ever stay where she put it? It was sliding down again, wispy and drifting around her face. He could see the desperation in her eyes. Brown? Sam dropped the shade again.

Leaning against the wall, he steadied himself, pain moving in waves through him. He couldn't help her and her son. Hell, he couldn't even get down the stairs and out to her car without making a major production of it.

He lifted the shade again. Brown eyes. Panicked. As he watched, she slowly opened the car door and got out. She leaned against the car, her head thrown back toward him, the slender curve of her throat achingly vulnerable. The sheen of perspiration dampened the pale slope offered to the sun. Her hand shaded her eyes as she slumped against the blinding white of the car. Listening, Sam stayed at the window.

"Mommy, what are we gonna do?"

She straightened, dropping her hand. "I don't know, Petey." Reaching into the car, she took her purse and opened it, yanking out a wad of tissue. Resolutely she blew her nose.

The dainty, forlorn honk kept Sam's hand on the shade.

"But, Mommy." Petey's voice rose in a wail.

"Shh, sugar, I'll think of something."

Sam heard the utter desolation in her voice. She hadn't the slightest idea what she was going to do, and probably no money to boot.

"Come on, Petey, we'll let the car rest for a minute while we get something cold. It'll start in a minute or two. I've just flooded the engine."

"Flooded prob'ly right." The boy nodded seriously.

Sam watched her narrow shoulders in the determinedly businesslike blue blouse droop. He knew that engine wasn't going to start, not in a minute, not in an hour, never without help.

Her pale legs in paler hose marched toward the house. The small figure at her side trudged with her to the front door, one hand in hers, the other with its thumb lodged firmly in his mouth.

Flicking the edge of the shade back and forth, Sam felt something stir in him, kicked up by the desperation and determination that shone in Hannah's eyes. But then he let the shade drop. He couldn't help her.

He flexed his left hand, working the muscles over and over, leaning against the wall, waiting for the muscle tremble in his legs to warn him that it was time to sit down or fall down. Then he would shave. Every day he made himself go through the motions. It would be cheating if he didn't.

The phone was cool in his right hand. He knew the number. Arnie had written down emergency numbers in his careful, precise handwriting. "Be easy to read, buddy," he joked. They were.

Holding the receiver under his chin, Sam thought for a minute and then tapped out seven digits.

In the stifling heat of her kitchen, Hannah swallowed the last of the iced tea and tried not to show her panic. She needed this job. What would she do if she didn't— No. Stop. Right now. She drew a deep breath. "Okay, Petey, let's go get our horses headed for town."

She saw the fright in Petey's eyes. He was scared, too.

"Mommy—"

"Come on, Petey," she said, forcing calm into her voice. "It's going to be all right. I promise." Hannah bowed her head for an instant and then opened the front door.

Behind the steering wheel again, she tried to think over the adrenaline pounding through her. Had she flooded the car? She knew she hadn't, not even in her haste to make her appointment.

"Yo, lady!"

She looked up. Leaning half out the window of his tow truck was a man whose wild red hair spritzed around his narrow face. One gold stud tastefully accented the gleam of a gold front tooth in a grin that seemed to go on forever.

"You got problems, huh, cookie?"

Petey's mouth fell open, and his thumb banged on the door handle. Wide-eyed, he stared at Hannah.

Hannah felt a little wide-eyed herself as the man hopped out and tapped on the hood of her car.

"Open 'er up, cookie, and we'll have you all set faster than a cat scratching litter."

Dazed, she pulled the hood release and sat, unable to think of anything. Rescued.

Petey scooted to the dashboard and peered under the gap between hood and car as the apparition banged and hammered.

"Yep, dead battery, sure enough. I'll fix 'er up quicker'n spit drying on a sidewalk." More banging and clanging. "Today's your lucky day, cookie!" He grinned around a wrench stuck in the corner of his mouth.

The dazzle of his gold tooth in the blazing sunlight snapped Hannah back to reality. Even miracles had to be paid for.

She leaned her head against the steering wheel and fought for breath. Slowly she reached for her purse. A little dizzy and disoriented, she opened her wallet.

She knew to the nickel how much money she had. She couldn't pay this man. Why was she even bothering to look?

"All done. Start 'er up, cookie, she oughta putt away smooth and sweet now."

Hannah started the engine. It putted away smooth and sweet. She closed her eyes for a second, afraid she was dreaming the steady sound of the engine. When she looked up again, the red-haired man was hopping back in his truck, a loopy grin on his face.

"Sir!" Hannah scrambled out of the car. "How much do I owe you?" she shouted.

He cupped his ear against the rattling noise of his own engine.

"How much?" Hannah shouted again.

With a thumbs-up gesture, he roared off, leaving Hannah with her mouth open. She couldn't take in what had just happened. She wouldn't think it had been real except for the steady, secure sound of her engine and the big-eyed stare of her son.

She shrugged at Petey as she returned to the car.

He leaned out the driver's window. "I told you, Mommy."

"What?" Hannah stopped with her hand on the door handle.

"My dragon. He made a spell. I told you he was real. Now you'll b'lieve me." He scooted over to his side and put on his seat belt with a satisfied nod of his head.

Bemused, Hannah looked down the road where the tow truck had disappeared.

She looked back at Petey. Just out of the corner of her eye, a small motion at the upstairs window of the house next door drew her attention.

Shimmering heat rose in waves toward her from the concrete.

The window shade had moved.

Hannah frowned, oddly disturbed.

As she watched, the shade flicked once more and then was still.

Chapter Two

For the second time, Hannah jabbed the doorbell. Once more the chimes bonged musically in the late-afternoon silence.

Looking at the shaded windows, she imagined echoes ringing through room after empty room.

But someone had to be there.

All day long that strange image of the barely disturbed shade had lingered, increasing her uneasiness. For Petey's sake, she'd known she couldn't ignore the misgivings plucking at her.

Heavy purple thunderclouds streaked with black and occasional yellow flashes were stacking up off in the west.

Whoever was hiding inside could just darned well come out and face her. She wasn't leaving. Hannah punched the doorbell and held her finger there.

The rubber end of a crutch shoved the door open. ''All right, damn it, you win. Lay off the bell.''

The door swung wide, and Hannah almost dropped her tuna-noodle casserole.

The grim-faced man looking down at her balanced on one crutch while the right held the door open and blocked the entrance. Only the wide shoulders forced up by the crutch pads and his long legs indicated the splendid physical presence he must have had once. Shaggy brown hair was slicked straight back from a fierce face, hawk nosed and thin in spite of the hard chin and prominent cheekbones.

In the shadowy recesses of the hall, a wheelchair angled in a doorway.

"What do you want?" His voice grated against her skin.

Hannah almost shoved the pink-and-white bowl at him and ran. She wanted to.

But the pain lurking deep in his dark hazel eyes rooted her to the unfriendly concrete steps, and she swallowed the pity that had held her momentarily speechless. In his eyes was the look of a man who'd been to hell and stayed there, burned to the bone.

"Here." She thrust out the casserole. "I'm your new neighbor."

"Yeah? So?" He hunched his powerful shoulders, bringing the right crutch upright. As he slid it under his armpit, its rubber tip slipped on the shiny terrazzo floor. "Damn."

She jerked the casserole back. He couldn't carry it. "Do you need some help?"

"No." As she leaned forward, he snarled. "Damn it, no!" The pain-gouged lines around his lips were white under the remnants of an old, old tan. The knuckles of his hands gripping the bars of the crutches were white, too, and marked with light scar lines. He steadied himself and ground out the syllables. "You're my new neighbor? Fine. You stay on your side of the fence, I'll stay on mine. We won't swap recipes, and I swear I won't borrow a cup of sugar. Okay? That way we'll be good neighbors." His lips were stretched thin. "Nice meeting you, neighbor."

He reached out and shut the door in her face, very quietly, very gently.

Hannah stared at the oak door panels. She looked down at the tuna casserole. The potato chips on top were still crisp. She'd cooked two. There was no room to freeze this casserole in the wretchedly small refrigerator that came with the house. She took a deep breath and banged the doorbell with her fist.

The door jerked open. "You." His scowl deepened the grooves in his face.

"Me." Hannah held the dish in a death grip. "I made this for you." Even in his ruined body, he radiated a force that unnerved her.

"You shouldn't have wasted your time. I don't want it." Hostility scored the scratchy voice. His hand clenched the heavy door edge. "I don't need it." Then, frowning and as if he'd reluctantly recalled civility, he added, "Thanks."

"Look," Hannah said, feeling like the world's biggest fool but determined not to lug the unwanted casserole back to her kitchen, at least not before she'd found out what she needed to know. "I don't have room for this in my refrigerator. It barely holds milk and margarine as it is. Anyway, Petey and I already have one for our supper."

He was reaching again for the doorknob.

Hannah knew she was a syllable away from babbling, but plowed on, hating the necessity that made her intrude. "You have to take it, or it'll just go to waste. Can't I just put this in your freezer? You might want it sometime? Need it?" She fumbled for words, made awkward by his obvious desire to have her vanish in a puff of smoke, yet caught by pity and the pain she'd seen under his fierce hostility.

Caught, too, by the glimpse of the man he must have been before—before whatever had turned him inside out and hung him out to suffer in a shell of himself.

In spite of every impulse telling her to run, she persisted, brushing away the hair drifting down into her eyes. "It'll keep. You could warm it up for tomorrow."

"*Neighbor,* do I have to spell it out for you? All I need from you is to be left alone! That's it. That's all. Not a damned thing more. Okay?" Anger sparked his eyes.

Despite the strength in his arms and shoulders where muscles had clearly been developed by carrying the greatest part of his weight, he looked as though he needed a good meal, Hannah thought. Under his loose, unbuttoned shirt, she caught a glimpse of skin stretched over ribs. He was wearing navy cotton gym shorts, and his long legs, legs that looked as though they'd once been heavily muscled, were thin in the leather straps and metal bands that supported them and clamped around his knees. Narrow white scars crisscrossed the light brown hair of his thighs and calves.

If he were a tomcat she'd found beside the road, she'd have dragged him home and given him a saucer of milk and a warm spot in the sun.

But there was a throttled-down power simmering in him that told her he was the kind of man she'd be better off walking a country mile to stay clear of.

Like a stray tom confused and maddened by pain, this man looked as though he'd shred her helping hand to ribbons.

"Mommy!"

Hannah turned and saw Petey's face edging around the bright red hibiscus bush at the side of the house. He was looking up at the tall man as though he'd seen one of the seven wonders of the world.

"Just a minute, Petey, please. I'm almost finished talking with our—neighbor." Hannah smiled at her son. Five minutes, and he'd found spiderwebs and dirt. A chameleon perched on his hand, quiveringly still.

Looking back at the silent man, she tried once more. She'd never felt so clumsy in her life. "Look, I promise Petey and I aren't going to pester you to death." She smoothed her palm down her bleached-white denim skirt. "I wanted to thank you for your help this morning. You called the tow truck for me, didn't you?"

Unblinking, Sam held her gaze.

He'd been right. Her eyes were brown, whiskey brown, like her hair.

He'd pulled his shades down to shut her and her son out, and now she was at his front door. He didn't want her pity, and he didn't want her thanks. And he didn't want her damned tuna casserole.

Deliberately, not looking away from those soft eyes, he lied. "I don't know what you're talking about."

A megawatt grin spread across the boy's small face.

Sam saw the flicker of disbelief on her face. Let her think what she wanted. As long as she left him alone. As long as he didn't have to watch her and her son and feel the deep-down gut-wrenching pain of being dragged into their lives. He'd have thought it was sheer nosiness that kept her glued to his doorstep, except there was a look in her eyes that made him figure she had her own reasons for ringing his doorbell, and thanks were the readiest excuse. Just so she let him alone.

But she was so damned persistent.

"My car wouldn't start. A man in a tow truck showed up and jump-started my car. He took off before I could pay him." Long fingers twisted up a spiral of that cloudy-soft hair as she stared at him. "I thought you might have seen my car and called the truck." She glanced up to the front of the house. "I owe someone for the repair."

"Not me." Sam edged the door forward. His leg muscles were cramping and knotting with spasms. He had to sit down or fall down, and he didn't fancy the idea of collapsing in a heap at her feet. "Check it out with the towing company."

Sweat was breaking out on his forehead as the spasms ran up his back, and his thigh muscles turned to jelly. He took a deep breath and clutched the door.

He had to get to his chair.

"I did. Someone named Louie told me everything was taken care of. I thought you might know something about it."

Through the haze of pain, Sam saw her puzzled expression and knew he had to get rid of her immediately. "No," he forced out through his dry lips. "You must have talked to the wrong guy." His sweaty hand slipped down the door edge as cramps convulsed his fingers.

One of his crutches clattered to the floor.

And then Sam felt her slim shoulder under his arm and held on as she took part of his weight. Her narrow hand gripped his firmly, her palm small under his. And between them the damned tuna-noodle dish bumped up warm against his bare skin.

"I'm okay," he said through clamped-down teeth.

"Right," she murmured with a note in her voice that made him look at her in spite of the pain pounding over his body like wild horses' hooves. "Don't worry, I'm not helping you." There was a rueful sweetness in the voice that had spun its magic for him night after night as he'd lingered in his dark garden.

He couldn't yield to its spell. "My chair."

"Petey? Can you come here, sugar?"

The boy warily stepped over the threshold and clutched a fold of his mother's skirt.

"Everything's okay, honey, but could you take this casserole and go get that chair for me?" She gestured with her head to the wheelchair, and the smell of shampoo and vanilla came to Sam with the brush of her hair against his arm.

His fingers clenched on her shoulder. Her apple green blouse was smooth and silky under his fingers. Pain and memory lashed his body, and he inhaled heavily.

In a whisper her warm breath touched his face, and he looked down into her uptilted face. "Hang on, Petey'll be right back. You're not going to fall." Her big brown eyes were soft with understanding.

An understanding he hadn't asked for and didn't want.

"I can make it." Sam forced himself to straighten and take a step.

"Of course you can." Her voice was husky, something moving in it like a song heard far off, an impression of notes trembling in air.

He shrugged her arm away and thrust his legs forward. Silently cursing the muscles that refused to obey, he compelled them finally to move on willpower alone and hoped they wouldn't betray him.

His legs buckled. But she moved in closer and stepped with him, her hip bumping his gently, and then the boy was there with the wheelchair, and Sam sank down into it with a grunt, closing his eyes.

The fragrance from her hair lingered faintly around him like winter sunrise, just barely there on the horizon.

His shaking hands flattened against the thigh muscles that twitched spasmodically under his fingers.

He heard her light sigh, the brush of her skirt against her leg.

A tentative tap on his arm brought his eyes open.

"I got your crutch." With the wooden structure looming over his head, Petey rested his chin on one handgrip and looked worriedly through the bars at Sam. "You want it now?"

"Yeah." Sam took the crutch and laid it across his legs with the other. "Thanks." The twitches were slowly subsiding, but sweat still poured down his back. Why hadn't he used the chair in the first place? Had he hoped—no. He didn't hope for anything anymore. Hadn't. Wouldn't.

He didn't want to look at Hannah, so he watched Petey's quick, curious glances around the foyer, the way he stayed at Hannah's side, his thumb in his mouth.

"Um, look, I'll go put this in your freezer, all right?"

Sam nodded.

"Back through here?" Her sandals shushed against the floor as she moved to the kitchen.

Her hips swayed slightly under the short denim skirt, and, in spite of his pain, his gaze was drawn to the pale flash of her bare legs in the deepening gloom of the hall. She and Petey disappeared around the corner, and the hall seemed darker and emptier.

Sam hesitated a moment, breathing deeply, listening to the murmur of her voice, the sounds of life stirring in the big kitchen. So much for his good-neighbor policy.

He was going to have to tell Arnie he couldn't stay. The rehab center would be better. Impersonal.

Using his palms, Sam slapped the wheels of his chair forward, propelling himself rapidly into the kitchen.

Twin faces of dismay met him. Hannah and Petey were standing in front of the open door of his refrigerator, the pink dish still in Hannah's hands. The glaringly bright bulb gleamed down on three bottles of beer and a white plastic container of days-old chili.

"You must be broker than us," Petey commented, frowning worriedly. "You'll just have to make do, I guess. That's what mommy says we gotta do."

"Petey!" Hannah shut her eyes and tried vainly to become invisible, prayed she would open her eyes and find herself anywhere else but standing in this enormous, sterile kitchen with her son spelling out their poverty to this man who quite obviously would like to send both of them speedily to the devil.

"Prob'ly why you don't got your lights on, huh?" Petey leaned against Sam's armrest.

"Petey, please!" Heat flooded Hannah's face. "We're leaving. I promised, Mr., uh, our neighbor, we wouldn't make pests of ourselves."

"Sam Dennehy." His long arm flipped on the light switch and recessed lighting bloomed.

"Excuse me?" Hannah blinked.

The man was like one of those Greek temples still awesome and splendid in its ruins. His face wore the map of some terrible suffering.

She glanced desperately at the casserole. She'd shove it in the fridge, and she and Petey could leave. This man with his empty refrigerator and empty life was no threat to her son.

"Sam." His scratchy deep voice was resigned and filled with infinite patience. "I'm your neighbor, Sam Dennehy."

"This is my mommy," Petey offered, tucking his head under the armrest of Sam's chair and peering up. "You know my name. I done told your dragon."

"Petey, that's enough, really!" Hannah flushed brighter as Sam's eyes rested on her, those deep, deep hazel eyes with their shadows.

"I know your son's name, but not yours." Sam wheeled closer.

Hannah wouldn't have believed a man sitting in a chair could shrink a room just by being in it. All the energy in the room focused on him, on the knife blade cheekbones, the thin face, focused and hummed like the motor of a powerful car engine. It was all submerged power, and the more unsettling as a result. She didn't even want to think of what he must have been like. He made her nervous in ways she couldn't identify. Hannah backed up, bumping into the corner of the kitchen table. She abandoned the despised casserole there. "Hannah Randall. Come on, Petey, we're going home." She snagged his hand and shifted toward the doorway.

Even though Sam had slanted his chair in her direction, even though she knew she was overreacting to that humming force, everything would have been fine.

But Florida Power and Light yielded to the summer storm that had threatened all afternoon and now suddenly boomed around them. All the lights flickered off. Outside, lightning hissed and crackled.

Hannah felt the hairs on her arm rise with the buzzing electricity and reached out for Petey.

Instead, she touched the hard, bare chest of Sam, felt the drumming of his heart under her fingers, and in his face outlined by a ripping crack of lightning saw such a look of raw hunger and despair that she felt as though the lightning had seared her from head to toe. In that dazzling brilliance, his hand rose slowly, swimming up out of the dark and touched her face, brushed the corner of her mouth, and then darkness swallowed him up. But his index finger lingered on her lower lip, where everything in her body suddenly centered and pulsed.

The room was silent, the motor of the air-conditioning off, and in the strangeness of that instant, Hannah forgot to breathe. Then, as breath came rushing back, she swung her arm out for Petey and touched his shoulder.

Sam Dennehy's harsh voice came out of the blackness and scratched along her nerve endings. "It's an electrical storm. Don't touch anything metal, the refrigerator or light switches. It'll blow over quickly."

He was a darker shadow at the window, opening the shades to the dazzle of the storm. The rubber wheels of his chair whooshed, and Hannah heard a drawer open, heard him rattle in the drawer before another booming crack deafened her. Petey's hand slipped into hers. White-hot Z's of lightning and deep blackness stitched through the kitchen.

The flashlight beam shone on Petey's face and then shot up to hers. "Why don't you sit down? I'll see if there are some candles in the pantry." The flashlight circled the kitchen table.

Hannah sat. Petey sat. As Sam and the flashlight disappeared behind a door, she shuddered and rubbed her hand against her thigh. Her mouth felt swollen, and her fingers still burned, burned.

Wheels whooshed in her direction again. "Here we go."

Dark-adjusted, her eyes could now see the man behind the flashlight beam held under his arm. Patches of shadow and light shining in his remarkable eyes.

He plunked the big flashlight down on the counter in back of him. It beamed a wide arc onto the table and the wall. "Did you ever camp out?" Looking at Petey, Sam rolled up to the table and stuck four fat white candles on top of a couple of cans of soup and a small metal platter.

"No." Petey's voice quavered as another zip of lightning cracked in the backyard.

"You never sat by a camp fire and told ghost stories?" Sam's voice was comfortingly patient.

Petey shook his head. "Don't like scary stories."

Hannah wrapped him tightly in her arms. She'd go camping with him.

She watched as Sam's shadow loomed large against the wall. As he shifted his weight to reach into his shorts pocket, the clingy jersey pulled against his thigh. An image of what he might have looked like.

Hannah shut her eyes.

"Well, we're going to have an indoor camp fire. Sort of. You'll like it. Everything's special by candlelight." He snicked a match against the side of a box, and the yellow flame licked at the candle wicks until the widening pool of light pushed the shadows back toward the wall.

Hannah welcomed the friendly candlelight. It vanquished the spell that had fallen over her since the moment her fingers had brushed against his taut skin in the dark and trembled to his thundering heartbeat. And then that searing lightning.

"Ms. Randall—"

"Hannah," she murmured. "Unless that's too neighborly?" She made her teasing light, using it to dispel her memory of that moment.

He shrugged, his shadow behind him echoing his movement. "Yeah, well, I like my privacy."

Petey leaned his head against Hannah. "You got your dragon for company. Does he stay outside in the rain?"

Hannah saw Sam's baffled look, but before she could explain, Sam leaned closer to Petey. Closer to her. With the air-conditioning shut down, the room seemed hot, airless.

"Truthfully?"

Petey nodded. "You always gotta tell the truth. I do." He glanced at Hannah.

"Truthfully I don't know." Like the candles on the table, Sam's small, rueful smile chased the shadows from his face. He touched the metal platter with his index finger. "What do you think?"

Hannah felt Petey squirming in her lap as he thought. His heels thumped against her knees.

"I think." Petey looked up at Hannah and stopped. "I think," he went on earnestly, "that a real dragon would not like this storm. I think he would go inside." Petey swiveled his head against her, looking to the dark corners of the room.

Hannah sighed. If they stayed any longer, Sam-with-the-haunted-face was going to know everything about her and Petey except her social security number and bra size. Glancing at Sam, she revised her last thought. He didn't look as though he'd missed anything about her so far. Hunger stirred in his bleak eyes. Her face flushed.

"Mr. Dennehy—"

"Sam," he mocked her, his expression reminding her of what she'd said.

"You're stuck with us. I'm sorry."

"Yeah, me too." He put his elbows on the table and folded his arms. Candlelight made yellow flecks in the green and brown of his eyes. "But here we are, *neighbor.*"

"I'm sorry," Hannah repeated helplessly, "but I didn't expect something like this and, the truth is, Petey and I haven't eaten since one o'clock this afternoon." She glanced at the still-warm tuna noodles. Her stomach rumbled, underlining her words. She knew her face was pink with embarrassment and something else.

"I had crackers and milk at the day care preschool. Mommy went to see about her job. I was s'posed to see if I liked the school. I did not." Petey wiggled again. "I only liked the snacks."

One dark brown eyebrow lifted. "You want to share my chili?"

He had to be kidding her. Hannah flinched as she remembered the crusted brown container in his refrigerator. Maybe not, she reconsidered as she looked at his gaunt face. He was a man who hadn't laughed in a long time. Even the smile he'd given Petey looked almost new.

"I think the tuna's still edible." She pushed the casserole fractionally in his direction. Her stomach rumbled again as the smell of cheese hit her nose. "Since you're stuck with us—and it—" she pointed to the dish, smiling a little at his expression "—you could get rid of all three of us if you'd tell me where you keep your plates."

Sam watched the candlelight softening the worry lines in her forehead, the slip-slide of wispy hair around her smooth face and the drowsy smile on her son's mouth. The three of them were linked by the light against the darkness.

But they weren't linked. He shook his head. He had no right to that small community of two. Loss and emptiness clawed at him with a ferocity he'd almost forgotten, twisting and biting. He doubled his fist, reminding himself with its weakness and cramping pain, letting it punish him.

Too many memories rushing out of the darkness as he looked across the table at Hannah and her son.

"We could eat while we're waiting for the storm to wind up. Unless—" she paused, anxiety creeping into her voice "—you want to toss us out in the storm?" She slid the casserole a tiny bit closer to him.

"No." Sam watched her slim index finger poke the dish toward him. He wished he could just pitch it, the boy and Hannah right out his front door. The thought scampered through his brain and tempted him. "I won't do that." He clenched his fist tighter, letting the cramps move up his arm.

"Want to tell me where you keep plates and forks?" Her smile was hesitant.

"Not really. What I *truthfully* want—" He stopped, remembering the light skin of her fingers against his skin, the surprising jolt that had pulsed through him in the darkness. Then he continued, brutally and coldly ignoring the hurt in her expression, "What I want, *truthfully,* is my house to myself." There was a bitter satisfaction in seeing her chin tremble.

It was as though he'd crossed some invisible line she'd drawn. She jerked to her feet, holding Petey tight to her. Her sudden movement dislodged one of the combs securing her hair, and it clattered onto the table, the small noise as loud in that moment as a cannon shot. "You've got it, Mr. Dennehy." With her hip she shoved the chair under the table, grabbed her comb with her free hand and jammed it into her hair, wincing as the teeth stabbed her scalp. "We'll be out

of here as soon as I can reach your front door." Her chin
lifted defensively.

Her mortification touched off the irritation that had
gnawed at Sam since she'd landed on his doorstep. His
emotions had been like the flat line on a heart monitor for
so long, that, caught by surprise, he almost didn't recog-
nize the boiling rush as anger. Angry with her for invading
his solitude and yanking him out of his safe numbness, angry with himself for looking at her and noticing her fragile
sweetness, Sam lashed out. "Not a minute too soon for
me!"

"I understand. Please accept my apologies." Her voice
shook slightly.

Although her words were shaded with exquisite politeness, Sam saw the withdrawal in her face. That was what he
wanted after all, so why did her chilly expression tick him
off? It was as though she'd lanced a boil and nastiness was
erupting from him with a virulence he couldn't control.

"I didn't ask you over, I didn't ask for your help and God
knows I didn't ask for your damned tuna noodles!" Sam
shoved the pink-and-white dish back over the table, his anger translated into the rocking, careening movement of the
casserole. It spun past the candles, skidded to the edge of the
table and crashed onto the bare floor.

Macaroni noodles burst skyward. One plopped into a
candle. With a roasting hiss, the wick sputtered out. A
chunky piece of tuna clung just above Hannah's left breast,
strings of brownish sauce sliding down and congealing on
the delicate curve.

She had a stunned, hurt look on her face that stopped him
cold.

"Mommy!" Petey wailed. "I want to go home!"

"So do I, sugar."

Her eyes never left Sam's face, and he felt like something
she'd wipe off the bottom of her shoe. He wanted to say
something, anything, but the outburst had drained him.

His hand was shaking. All that emotion. It had been like
the storm, fierce, electrical and fast moving, banging out of

nowhere and then moving on, leaving devastation in its wake.

Snugging her son securely on her hip, she carefully scraped off the piece of tuna and sauce before speaking. A smear of grease made the blouse cling to her skin. The shiny material pressed against the small bump of her nipple.

He couldn't look away.

She spaced her words for emphasis, but they were low and controlled in spite of the anger. "You know something, Mr. Dennehy? You're so afraid that someone's going to feel sorry for you. Believe me, I don't. There are worse things than wearing braces and riding a wheelchair. Whatever is eating you up inside is much worse. And that wound doesn't show."

With that, she laid the tuna chunk precisely in the center of his table.

In the candlelight, Sam saw the bloodless white of her face as she walked blindly past him out of the kitchen. He reached out his hand to stop her just as lightning lit up the room with blue-white brilliance before plunging them back into darkness.

His outstretched, straining fingers grasped only emptiness.

Chapter Three

Heavy, wet air from the opened door swirled around Sam. His heart was pounding. Sick regret rose in his throat. His poisonous mood and ruthless words had driven the woman and child out into the storm. He hadn't meant to smash the casserole, hadn't meant for her to go racing into the lightning-split night.

She hadn't raced, the stern judge in his brain reminded him. What had he thought she'd do? He hadn't *thought*. There was the problem. No one could be expected to stand still for the kind of hostility he'd been spitting out. But she should have stayed, he thought uselessly. And put up with more nastiness just to have a port in a storm?

Looking out at the windy darkness and fallen branches, Sam wanted to smash that ruthless voice in his head. Unforgivable. Inexcusable. He cursed himself up one side of the barn and down the other, such rage at his behavior flooding him that he was shaking.

What had been going through his mind?

Under the rain-soaked transparency of her blouse, he saw the outline of lace and, in the middle, the pale rose of her nipples, blooming like tea roses in a wet, green field. She was so small and delicate.

"Why don't you—" She stammered.

"I'd better go on back—"

Their words bumped together. Sam started over. "I'll go on back now that I know you're both all right." His mouth was dry. Sitting in his chair, looking up at her, he couldn't avoid seeing the faint flutter of her breasts as she spoke or the pale rose spreading up her neck and to her face as she intercepted his glance.

"*I* was going to ask you if you wanted a second chance at the tuna casserole." She laughed. "Mine is in the oven, so it should be warm. It's still early." Shadows of exhaustion washed her skin.

Sam started to say, yes, he'd have supper with them, that, yes, for the first time in a year and a half, he was hungry, really, truly hungry, yes—

And then, sweet, sweet, her voice glided over him, silk against his raw nerves. "Please stay."

Sam gripped the spokes of his wheelchair until he could give the only possible answer. He knew better than to stay. "That's not such a good idea."

"But—" Her tired brown eyes reflected her confusion.

She disturbed him at a primitive level he couldn't protect. And he had to. No mountaintops, but no canyons, either. No more wild soaring into limitless blue for him. Never again.

He'd lashed out at her to put distance between them. That hadn't worked. And he hadn't, when push came to shove, been able to keep his distance, so his reply, though more gently delivered, was kin to his earlier slamming of the door in her face. "I can't."

Sam looked away from the brown eyes and soft mouth that tempted him to forget about the price a man paid for risk taking and wanting the impossible. He massaged his leg just above the knee brace. "Thanks, anyway."

Petey drooped at her side, his eyes following Sam's hands as they massaged the knotting muscles under the leather straps. "Those are funny Band-Aids." His arms were wrapped around Hannah's bent knee, his cheek resting on her thigh where his arms had bunched her skirt. "Mommy gets G.I. Joe Band-Aids for me. You can have one for your oobie."

Sam wanted to see if that strip of gleaming skin where Petey's cheek rested was as smooth as it looked. Wanted those fingers stroking her son's rumpled hair touching him.

"Nice of you to offer, kiddo, but I'd be real surprised if you had one big enough for me."

"Does your oobie hurt all the time?" Petey commiserated.

Sam valued the truth as much as anyone, but for the second time found himself lying to this dynamic duo. That solemn little face looked as though it had seen enough unpleasant garbage. "Not often."

Looking up, Sam saw the look in Hannah's eyes. Her mouth didn't exactly curve up in sympathy, but it came close enough to it to tell Sam she knew he was lying. And why. She didn't say anything, though. He was glad. The boy didn't need to know how painful reality could be. Not yet. Time enough for the kid to learn those lessons.

And past time to hightail it out of here. He gestured to the door. "Will you get that?"

"Of course." She opened the door and the smell of the world made clean and new rushed in.

"So long." Sam looked out at rain-washed greens so bright they made his eyes ache. The evening sky, impossibly blue after the fury of the storm, was a miracle of pinks and greens glowing and deepening as the sun slipped past the earth's curve.

"Bye, Mr. Sam." Petey wiggled his fingers. "You oughta stay, though."

"Yeah, maybe." Sam turned his back and rocked his chair off the curb and down to the driveway. The way back stretched on forever.

Hannah hadn't meant to watch him until he turned into his own entry, but she couldn't look away from the solitary figure slowly wheeling toward his empty house and its shaded windows.

When Sam finally disappeared, she turned to Petey and patted his stomach. "So, what's it going to take to fill up that tiger I heard growling under there?"

What it took was a bottomless bowl of cereal. Like Sam, Petey rejected the hapless casserole. Now, slurping and spilling, Petey kept shaking out raisins and flakes in a futile attempt to make milk and cereal come out even. When he finally gave up and headed out the kitchen door, Hannah called him back. "Hey, sugar, what did you forget?"

"A kiss?" He lifted on tiptoe, milky mouth pursed.

"Well, that, too." Hannah kissed him.

"Oh." He looked at the kitchen table. It looked like a map of the Thousand Lakes dotted with raisin islands.

"*Oh* is right." Hannah laughed and tossed him the dishrag. His fanny bobbed as he swung his short arms like windshield wipers, erasing the map.

"Going out now." He trotted to the screen door.

"Okay, but stay in the yard, sugar. I'm going to see if I can strip the wallpaper in the bathroom before we take our baths. And then—"

"And then we finger paint the walls!"

"Yep." Hannah closed the screen door behind him. She'd fall asleep standing up before this day was over. "Stay close so you can hear me, okay?" she called as he jumped down the back porch steps and out into the wet yard.

Upstairs, Hannah lifted the bathroom window. She'd changed into shorts, sneakers and an old, V-necked cotton T-shirt to work in.

Down below her in the yard, Pete's voice lilted up and down. From this angle she could also see the light from what she now knew was Sam's kitchen. She smiled. He'd left the blinds open.

His gritty loneliness tugged at her. No matter what he said, though, he'd come out in the storm to make sure she and Petey were safe. She couldn't remember the last time anyone had been worried enough about her to try to protect her. She was usually the one who did the looking after.

Warmth moved lazily through her. Sam had been concerned enough about her and Petey to break his self-imposed isolation.

Keeping part of her attention on the sounds her son was making, noticing with another part of her mind that Sam had turned off his kitchen light, Hannah pried up the edge of the wave-patterned wallpaper. She didn't have another interview until Friday, so she should be able to strip and paint the bathroom. If she were lucky, she could get the whole room stripped tonight. If not, well, there was always tomorrow.

She was lucky.

Out in the yard, Petey shook the heads of the tall sunflowers and laughed as water poured down on him. He settled himself carefully on the tree stump as he heard the familiar creaking and clanging and smelled the smoky breath. He had a lot to tell his dragon tonight.

"Hey, there," Petey whispered. He still wasn't real sure the dragon wouldn't fly off, so he didn't want to startle him.

"Hay's for horses, kid," said the dragon so low Petey could hardly hear him. His red eye was dull.

"That's a joke, right?"

"Yeah, just an old chestnut." The dragon sighed.

More jokes. Petey shook his head. Dragons were as bad as grown-ups. "Guess what? Me and Mommy met a funny man in a tow truck and we visited Sam, and I didn't like him *at all* right away, Sam, I mean."

A tree frog chirped.

"Sometimes I don't like him very much, either," the dragon said on a long sigh. "He's not a nice guy. Better for you both if you and—" the dragon paused, his voice rasping "—your mommy stay away from him."

"But *later,*" Petey insisted, hoping the dragon wouldn't blast him away for arguing, *"later,"* I liked him a whole bunch."

"Oh."

Petey thought about the look in Sam's eyes when they'd all been cozy in the kitchen. "He's sad, I think, prob'ly."

The dragon didn't answer for a long, long time. "Yeah," he finally agreed.

His voice faded away, and they sat in silence. Petey leaned against the fence and decided he'd like to camp out in the yard. He could talk to the dragon all night long then.

A loud crash and thump came from the dragon's spot. Petey jumped and looked through the peephole as hard as he could, but he couldn't see anything. His dragon was still there. Petey could hear raspy groans that scared him.

"You okay?" Petey stuck his thumb in his mouth and waited.

There was no answer.

Without a backward glance, Petey sprinted home.

Hannah heard Petey's shrieks and ran down the stairs so fast her momentum bounced her sideways against the wall at the bottom. Her heart was banging against her ribs.

The screen door banged. "Mommy! Mommy! You gotta help him," Petey screamed. "He's died!"

"Petey, what are you talking about?" Hannah steadied him, cradling his face as she searched frantically for blood. "What's going on, sugar?" Her legs were wobbly with fear.

Petey was okay, but something was badly wrong to put him in this quivering state. "Slow down and tell me, all right, honey?" She tried to smile, but her lips were shaking as much as her hands.

Petey's hands were pulling on her shorts. "Help him! He don't talk no more. You gotta go!" Jumping up and down, tears streaming from his face, Petey pointed to the house next door. "Hurry!"

Hannah thought as fast as she could. What could have happened to Sam? She didn't know his medical condition. She remembered his earlier strain, the effort he'd exerted to get to her house, and she was frightened. "Petey, you stay here. In the kitchen, hear me? *Don't* leave, and don't follow me. This is important, sugar, so you have to help by minding me, okay?"

Petey nodded anxiously.

"I'll be right back. See? I'm setting the timer, and I'll be back before it dings." Hannah twisted the dial and set it for ten minutes. She could count on Petey's staying still that long.

Her mouth was dust dry. Whatever had happened, she didn't want Petey seeing it.

Hannah bolted out the back door and through the narrow grassway between the two houses to the front walk. There was no way to get from her backyard to the other yard, but she thought she saw, just off the driveway, a self-locking gate that gave entry to the backyard.

Her trembling hands couldn't move the stiff metal lock until she used the hem of her T-shirt to help her get a tighter grip and wiggle the bolt free. Her heart thudding so hard she shook all over, Hannah hurried to the backyard.

Under the oak tree a dark shape lay collapsed on the wet ground. She wished she had a flashlight. Close up, she could see Sam bent double, his eyes closed. His crutches lay next to him, his wheelchair back toward the patio off the kitchen door.

She pressed her fingers gently to his neck. There, the steady thumping against her hand calmed her.

He was alive.

Hannah gave a silent prayer of thanks to whatever gods looked after prickly, stubborn, *dumb* men who thought they were better off keeping people at arm's length.

The prickly, stubborn, *dumb* man lying in front of her opened his eyes. "You again." His voice was filled with agony.

"I know." She managed a smile, grateful he wasn't still unconscious. As big as he was and with his injuries, she wouldn't have dared to move him. "We've got to quit meeting like this."

Even in the dark, she saw his eyes glitter. "Fate, I reckon." A groan slipped out.

Hannah touched his face, afraid to bump his arms or neck. Her fingers trembled again. "Do I call an ambulance?"

"I don't know yet. My back's gone out, and my muscles are spazzing like crazy, but I don't think anything's broken." He levered up with one arm. "Hell and damnation." His arm quaked beneath his weight. He scowled at her. "Any chance you can get me in the wheelchair if I can stand at all?" Sweat beaded on his forehead and slid down his hard cheekbones.

Still shaking, Hannah exhaled in relief. "Well, tough guy, if you get even semivertical, I'll get you in that chair. I'm stronger than I look, believe me."

His frown was skeptical. "You'll have to be. I'm heavier than you'll expect."

Hannah thought about it. From the waist up, he was thin, but all muscle. His legs were convulsing. She couldn't count on his being upright for long. "Tell me what to do." Sympathy flooded her. "And how. I don't want to hurt you. Or twist your back."

He grimaced. "Don't worry. At this point, I won't even notice if you do. I don't want to call an ambulance." His voice was strained. "If I can get inside and lie down, take my medicine, I'll be fine." He slumped back.

"Do you want me to get your medicine first?" Hannah stood up.

Irritability underscored his voice. "No. I just want to get up off this damned ground! Hell, I hate lying here helpless like this." He glared at her. "Just get me in my chair, okay? Don't worry about anything else."

"Right." Hannah glared right back at him. Her emotions bubbled like a stew pot. Terror at seeing him unconscious, relief that he was alive and outrage that fate had condemned him to the kind of suffering he endured rushed her into careless speech. "Heaven forbid I should worry about you! I mean, any darned fool can see everything's peachy keen. You're sprawled like a log and can't move, you've got nothing but smells in your fridge, and when

someone has the nerve to offer help, you're about as friendly
as a grizzly bear. Golly gee, how could anyone possibly
worry about you? You've obviously got everything under
control!''

His expression closed off. "Right." He struggled to a sitting position.

Hannah wished she could take back every word. She
knew how humiliating it was to have to ask for help. She'd
never spoken like that to anyone. Southern-polite to the
core, she'd rather cover up than confront. Not a yeller and
a screamer, she'd exploded like a pressure cooker at this
helpless man.

No, not helpless. Definitely not that. So much control
radiated from Sam Dennehy, so much formidable will that
no one would dare label him helpless, not even flat on his
back.

He'd be a man who'd crawl over hot rocks to get where he
wanted.

Hannah pressed her hands against her stomach to keep
from reaching out and touching the lines contorted in his
face by the strength of his efforts.

He clenched his teeth together as he pushed himself up
onto his hip. "You've had your say. I can't argue with a
single word you've said. I know what I am." He flexed his
fingers, shaking out the cramps. "Can you, now that you've
gotten all that off your chest, bring my chair over here?''

"Yes." Subdued, Hannah got the chair and pushed it
over the bumpy ground through the heavy, wet grass. It was
hard work. No wonder his arms and shoulders were muscled. She was breathing hard when she stopped at his side.
"Now what?''

"Hang on a minute," Sam grunted. "Give me a second." He considered her slight figure. Close up and in her
brief shorts, she looked as though she'd blow away in a light
breeze, but she'd stood up to him and his damnable mood-
iness and never flinched. She had a strength all her own.
She'd need it because his legs were virtually useless until the
cramps stopped. If she dropped him—

She wouldn't. Sam didn't know where his certainty came from, but he knew he could count on her. He'd bet on it.

"Okay. Here's what you do." He motioned for her to come to his side. "You'll have to kneel down here next to me. Get your shoulder and back up under my arm. When I say so, you have to straighten up fast while I pull. We'll have to do it the first time." Sam hoped they could do it on one try. He was going to be bawling like a baby if he didn't get his pain pills and muscle relaxant.

"I'm ready." She positioned herself as he'd indicated. Smaller, sweetly curved, her smooth thigh was next to his. She dug her toes into the ground and waited, watching him closely with her soft brown eyes that made him ache with their reminder of what life might have been like for him except for one second's criminal stupidity. God couldn't send him enough pain to make up for what he'd done in that second.

"Look, don't think about how you're hoisting me, okay? Just heave me into the chair any way you can."

She nodded. Sam gripped her shoulder. Her bones were so delicate. His bulk would break her. He took a deep breath and nodded.

In one quick thrust, Sam pulled with his left arm just as Hannah rose, and between them he found himself launched jarringly into the chair. Every vertebra in his spine jolted. Sweat beaded on his forehead. He'd be okay now. He could get inside. He wouldn't need the damned ambulance. Wouldn't have to go back to the damned hospital. Over and over, he swore in a soundless stream as Hannah pushed him over the ground and into the kitchen.

"Where's your medicine?" Like blues in the night, her voice throbbed around him.

Sam opened his eyes. Tears clung to her eyelashes, and the pale oval of her face glimmered in front of him. "Upstairs. Bathroom," he managed to say before the pain took him.

Her bare feet made no sound, but he heard her banging open cabinets and drawers until she found the capsules, heard the rush of water as she filled a glass.

Water dripped on him. "Here, swallow." She popped two pills in his mouth. The level of water in the clear glass wavered as she held it to him.

Taking it, holding it with her cool, damp fingers tight around his, Sam gulped the pills greedily while the glass clinked like castanets against his teeth. Water spilled and ran down his face.

Her fingers brushed the sides of his mouth, a gentle touch that shivered through the fog of pain right down to the center of him. "I have to see about Petey. I'll be right back. Don't worry."

Sam lifted his finger, signaling he'd heard. "Wait," he muttered, trying to tell her not to come back, but she was running through his front door.

"I'll set up something so you can sleep down here," she called back. "You can't make it up to your bedroom. I'll just be a minute." Anxiety and compassion threaded the music of her voice and drew him once more.

Drifting in the welcome numbness of the pills, his hard-won defenses breached, Sam was tempted to dive into the warmth of Hannah Randall, drown in the sea of her and wash away his loneliness and pain.

He couldn't do that. She didn't deserve it. He couldn't ever forget that, no matter how much he wanted to.

God knew, he'd forfeited the chance for happy endings. Like the guy in the myths he'd read about in another life, he was doomed to have the eagle claw at his entrails over and over in endless punishment.

He was alone.

It was only what he deserved, he reminded himself as he wheeled himself wobbily to the staircase.

Hannah used up more time than she'd expected, and when she returned with Petey in tow, she saw the empty wheelchair turned over at the foot of the stairs.

"Idiot, idiot, crazy fool," she mumbled, wondering what she'd find upstairs.

Hannah took Petey's hand and led him to the Florida room that led off the hallway.

"He isn't died?" Petey's voice was frightened.

"No, sugar, he's okay, just sleeping. Come in here with me." Taking the liberty of turning on the television and flipping the channel selector, Hannah found a cable channel that was still showing children's programming. She took off Petey's shoes and settled him in the large chair facing the set. It had been so long since he'd seen TV that he wouldn't move. He smiled at her as she left the room, and then, enraptured, turned to the bright colors and movement.

Slowly Hannah climbed the stairs. She snapped on the hall light and pushed open the door to Sam's room.

Not a room. A cell. She hadn't noticed in her frantic search for his medicine, but the room was stripped of everything personal, anything that hinted of comfort.

An overhead fan revolved sluggishly over the figure supine on the twin bed, his arms stretched out to his sides.

Hannah wondered what it had cost him to pull himself step by step up the stairs and into this room. And why he'd thought it necessary to do so.

His long brown hair was soaked in sweat. She went into the bathroom and wrung out a cloth in cool water. Wiping his face, Hannah pushed the thick strands of damp hair back from his forehead.

Yearning to ease his pain and offer him comfort, Hannah smoothed the washcloth over him. As the thick strands of his hair clung to her fingers, something down deep inside her coiled, its tendrils quivering and winding through her with every beat of her heart.

Then his eyes opened, glittery in the shadowy room. In his raspy voice slurred now with drowsiness and medicine, he murmured, "You shouldn't have come back." His hand lifted and touched the curve of her ear, slid down the slope of her neck, hung in the V of her T-shirt.

His fingers were cool, his touch an ice that burned over her skin. "I said I would," Hannah breathed. Her blood was beating slowly and thickly in time with the revolving fan blades, their sluggish circling hypnotizing her into stillness.

"You shouldn't have," he repeated, his palm sliding to the back of her neck, drawing her down to him, his touch sliding, stroking over her arms, her neck, her mouth, branding her.

Hannah's knees buckled. His arms caught and braced her, wrapped around her with a strength she'd never known she was missing. Her lips brushed his neck as she slipped to the floor. His forefinger moved down her spine, slowly, slowly, to the flare of her hips, to the edge of her raggedy shorts, leaving fire behind, fire everywhere he touched. His glittery eyes watched her, engulfed her.

"Get out of here, Hannah Randall," he muttered, holding her tight to him as his palms smoothed over her thighs and brought her knee over him.

"Yes," Hannah said, not really hearing him, her skin leaping, fluttering under his restless fingers.

"Take your precious son and get away from me," he said groggily, his hands tightening around her shoulders as he half rose, his eyes wide and anguished.

Startled out of the spell his touch had woven around her, Hannah said, confused, "What do you mean?"

"Because I'm like that old king, the one who turned anything he touched into gold. He killed everything, everything he loved. I'm a destroyer, Hannah Randall, I destroy everything I touch—" his words ripped into the room "—so run as fast as if you had the hounds of hell biting at your heels. Because they are." His voice was raspy. "And for your own sake, don't look back."

His lips took hers, hungry and despairing and pulling her down into a world dark with yearnings she'd never known existed, where skin pulsed and hummed, and his mouth bound her with chains she'd never dreamed could be forged in a fire of touching and wanting.

His hands slid from her.

"Run, Hannah," he said in a barely heard voice, his head dropping to the pillow, his eyes closing. "While you can. Run before I destroy you, too."

Seg Michael, "Seven in a family of eleven... what a difference to the future ... he's a joke ... are you one. Kies through... every woman

Chapter Four

Twining in and out of the thready edges of Hannah's cut-offs, Sam's long fingers twitched in a restless, pain-filled sleep against her bare thigh. Except for the ceaseless scrabbling of his fingers clutching and pulling at the frayed strings, he lay still as death.

Hannah's lips still burned from his kiss. Their kiss. It hadn't been a one-sided moment. She had been led willingly into the darkness his mouth promised.

Her mind had fled before the urgency and passion in his touch. All that power she had earlier sensed in his kitchen and stepped back from had burst loose upon her and oh, she had wanted him. For that honeyed moment, she knew she had *wanted* more than she'd ever dreamed possible.

Lured by the hunger of his mouth against her, caught by the strength of his need, hers, she would have stayed wrapped in that dark enchantment.

But then he had dropped like a stone into medicine-induced sleep, and she had remained bemused by his side, held there by the frantic scrabbling of Sam's fingers crying out in a desperate language of their own against her humming skin.

Now, suddenly, jerking his left leg against her hip, his calf knotted and spasmed. Half expecting the spasms to wake Sam, Hannah waited, but he never moved. Just that twisting and cramping of his muscles moving with a will of their own. A monstrous will to distort his once-powerful legs while he lay unconscious and vulnerable. Tentatively she stretched out her hand and then withdrew it.

Unfair, Hannah thought, remembering his fierce rejection of help. He would hate for her to see him like this. She knew that as well as she knew her own name.

The hard outline of convulsing muscles was disturbing to watch, and again his leg jerked and leapt with a manic life of its own. She couldn't stand watching that merciless attack on him as he lay, sleep stunned, defenseless.

Touching his tensing calf, she sighed as the energy of contorted muscles under fine hair jerked under her palm and coursed through her. Her fingers tingled.

Interrupting the feathery hair under her hand, a thin webbing of scar tissue ran in slick lines against her fingers, mute testimony to horror endured and survived.

"Who are you, Sam Dennehy? What happened to you?" Hannah whispered in the quiet room as she watched the merciless attack of his body against his unconscious self. "And why did you think you had to warn me away from you? Dangerous? A destroyer? Not you," she scoffed, thinking about the look on his face when she'd opened her door to him and he'd leaned against her door for support.

"No, don't," she murmured in distress as his right leg now trembled and began a spasmodic dance of its own. "Ah, no," she said, no longer able to watch, and closed her hand over the bunching muscle.

Moving her fingers into the long muscle strands, Hannah slowly worked against the cruel twisting of his thighs and calves. Over and over, first one leg, then the other, kneading and prodding, she smoothed her aching palms and tired fingers against Sam's hot skin while she fought the brutal betrayal of his body.

For his sake, she hoped he remained unconscious. With the shield of his powerful personality and resolution smashed by pain and medication, she felt uncomfortably as though she were violating his privacy, and she didn't want him knowing she'd seen him like this. His vulnerability at this moment was too close to the helplessness of the hospital, and he'd given her a glimpse of the hell that had been for him.

She pulled the edges of his shirt together. "All right, so you'd hate for me to be doing this. Well, tough," she said through gritted teeth, and dug her thumbs deep into a resistant knot above his knee. "Oh, I don't blame you. I wouldn't want to be helpless, either, and I wouldn't want to be lying unconscious while someone stared at me, but there's nothing wrong, darn it, with letting someone help you!"

The knot didn't yield. "You don't have to be so stubborn." She shook her head, and a strand of hair caught at the corner of her mouth. Lifting her shoulder, she brushed it free. "You are stubborn, you know," she said as her fingers worked their way up his long leg, deeper into the knotted muscles, while the medication kept him unaware of her touch.

She rotated her palm at the outside edge of his gym shorts where the soft jersey shaped itself to his thighs. He must have spent long hours rehabilitating himself after whatever surgery had left its spidery trace on him.

He would have spent months rebuilding his shattered legs. What had all that time done to him? Had there been anyone by his side when he'd forced his body into a cruel discipline?

As she bent and flexed his knee, Hannah somehow thought Sam Dennehy had spent a lot of lonely hours. No sense of accomplishment gleaming in his hazel eyes. Nothing there but stay-away and pride.

Hannah shifted carefully on the bed, and her knee brushed a hard hipbone. Before his accident, his thighs would have been as big as his waist, she noticed, glancing at the narrow band riding just at the dip of his belly button.

Her wrist had fallen just there where the ridged slope of his stomach disappeared under faded blue. Looking at the corded muscles of his stomach, Hannah flushed. Her fingers stilled at the lower edge of blue.

His chest had been so hot against her when he'd pulled her down against him. His stomach had been flat and hard, and his heart had gone wild against her while his kiss stunned her into forgetting they were strangers. Even now, merely remembering, Hannah swallowed. Her skin tightened and heated.

Hannah shivered. Whatever she'd expected when she'd rung his doorbell, it wasn't this man with his gaunt face and shuttered eyes, this man who would just as soon have slammed his door on her.

Hannah thought about the way he'd avoided leaning on her shoulder until she'd stepped next to him, thought about his grudging acceptance of her help. "You're not just stubborn, Sam Dennehy, you're no better than a prickly old porcupine permanently bristled up!"

Her hand brushed the still-damp edge of his shorts, the same ones he'd worn earlier in the rain. "And you could have changed your clothes, too! Nobody asked you to come roaring into the storm after me. I wouldn't have taken Petey out if it was dangerous, no matter how mad at you I was. So it's your fault, you know, if you catch your death of pneumonia after a soaking like that," she scolded while she let anger and worry strengthen her weary hands and flow into Sam's spasming legs.

As the long minutes crept past in the gloom and quiet, Hannah remembered the nights she'd stayed up rubbing Petey's left leg after he'd overstrained it, remembered, too, Carl's sleepy annoyance when she'd slipped out of bed to go to Petey.

At least she'd been there for Petey.

Somehow she didn't think anyone, at least anyone who counted, had been there for Sam Dennehy in a long, long time.

Sam's muscles were smooth under her soothing fingers. His legs rested quietly under her hands. Hannah glanced down. Without her noticing, the spasms had ceased.

Her shoulders slumped, and she took a deep breath, brushing away a strand of hair from her cheek. Surprised by the slight trembling of her fingers, she extended them in front of her and studied their unsteadiness. She'd been more tense than she realized. Stretching them, she stared at Sam.

His face was too thin. His cheekbones jutted out with a sharpness that betrayed his lack of concern for food. Well, she'd seen the contents of his refrigerator. She didn't have to be a genius to conclude he wasn't interested in food.

Leaning forward to his angular face, Hannah smoothed the frown lines on his forehead. "Sam Dennehy, you're a fool not to take better care of yourself," she muttered. "Even a mangy old dog eats better than you do. You could phone for a pizza, at least. You could even get the grocery store to deliver! There's no excuse for your doing this to yourself!"

She pulled out the spread and laid it carefully across him. So painfully thin. Anger bubbled inside. "Sam Dennehy, if you don't care enough about yourself to eat right and come in out of the rain, why in the world should I worry about you?" She stood up. "So I'm not going to, that's what. You hear me?"

But he didn't hear, and she did worry.

Going downstairs to Petey, her hand trailing along the stair railing, Hannah tried to fit together the contradictory pieces of the puzzle that Sam Dennehy presented to her. She marveled at the will that had pulled him up these same stairs but let him neglect his well-being in other ways.

She still couldn't believe he'd struggled up to his bedroom. How would he manage in the morning when his sore muscles stiffened and refused to respond?

Trying to forget the glazed, lost look in Sam's eyes when he'd curled his lean fingers around her neck, Hannah went in to her son.

Petey lay curled on the couch, his thumb securely stuck in his mouth. His knees were drawn up to his chest. In a tidy, self-contained ball, he was as sound asleep as Sam.

"Oh, sugar," Hannah sighed. "Now what are we going to do?" She kneeled next to him and smoothed his hair. "We can't stay here all night, but I don't want to wake you up, and what about Sam tomorrow morning? What if he can't even get out of bed?" She laid her hand on Petey's soft cheek. "I wish he weren't so thin, sugar."

A tiny whistle escaped from Petey, and he sucked his thumb more firmly into his mouth.

Hannah looked up the dark stairwell. What if Sam couldn't even get a drink of water? What if he became ill during the night and couldn't get help? She glanced back at her sleeping son.

"Now listen, Petey, Sam Dennehy is a grown-up man. He'll be just fine. If he doesn't want to eat, that's his business, right?"

Petey snored.

"He doesn't want us around, anyway." Hannah tapped Petey's button nose. "So come on, honey, let's go home."

She slid her arms under Petey, ready to stand up, and then, glancing once more at the long stretch of stair, she imagined Sam pulling himself up one step at a time while he fought the cramping and pain in his body. Hannah slowly withdrew her arms from Petey.

She couldn't leave Sam while he was unconscious. She'd rather not stay in his house for all kinds of reasons, tiredness only the least of them.

But Sam lay in darkness, and she couldn't abandon him. That's all there was to it.

When he was awake with all his defenses in place, well, okay, he could make his own choices.

No big deal if she and Petey slept downstairs here on the couch. Before they'd moved, they'd slept often enough on friends' couches, and Petey was fine as long as she was near him.

She'd need a sheet or a blanket for Petey. Hannah hated the idea of searching through Sam's house, but she didn't want to go home and leave Petey alone without telling him where she'd gone. If he woke up, he'd call for her.

He'd be terrified if she didn't answer.

"Sorry, Sam, I know you don't want us here, and I don't want to be here any more than you want us, but I guess you're stuck with us again," Hannah mumbled as she stood up and tried to figure out where extra sheets or blankets might be.

Moving quietly through the upstairs hall, she looked in on Sam. Except for the slight movement of the spread over his chest, he was absolutely and frighteningly still as he lay on his back in the barren room.

Hannah slipped in and, checking for fever in the same way she always did with Petey before pulling out the thermometer, she touched Sam's forehead with her lips before she realized what she was doing.

His forehead was warm. Concerned, she touched him again. Warm, not hot. She didn't think he had a fever.

His skin was smooth against her mouth, and the smell of rain lingered in his hair. He moved. His head turned to her, and his cloudy hazel eyes opened and looked right at her.

As though she'd swooped down a steep, circular playground slide and thumped right on her bottom, Hannah felt as though the wind had been knocked out of her.

How had she ever thought Sam Dennehy was defenseless?

Hazel eyes locked on hers, he raised his palm to her cheek.

He never touched her, but the burn of air against her skin sent her heart racing and bumping, and all the while he watched her with something desperate shining out of those drugged eyes. And then the light went out and his eyes closed.

Shaken, Hannah backed out of his room.

She and Petey were going home.

Her fingers gripped the edge of the door. There had been no awareness in Sam's eyes. Just that fierce eagle glare staring at her, fighting the pull of unconsciousness and losing.

She couldn't go home and leave him to fend for himself.

Her heart still thumping erratically and leaving her breathless, Hannah freed her grip and headed down the hall. In the hall closet she found sheets and extra pillows. Since Sam's house was air-conditioned and cool, she took a blanket for Petey.

Downstairs, snuggled next to Petey under the sheet and blanket, Hannah watched the stairs uneasily until the faint hum of the air conditioner lulled her into uneasy sleep and she drifted into a world where the dim, swiftly striding figure of Sam followed her in and out of shadows, pursuing steadily no matter how fast and far she ran, the steady rhythm of his footsteps echoing her heartbeat.

And his raspy voice calling after her down the alleyways of dreams, "Run, Hannah, run."

Sam woke to the sound of the ceiling fan and voices.

Hannah.

A confusing memory of her wide brown eyes staring at him with concern sifted through his impressions of the night. A faint, teasing remembrance of cool lips touching his face. Like glittery flecks in fool's gold, shining and false, the dreamlike impressions mixed with what he knew for sure had happened.

The climb up the stairs. After that, a jumble, nothing clear. He couldn't trust his memories to tell him the difference between what he'd imagined and what had really happened.

Even though he'd apologized, Hannah wouldn't have been concerned about him, not after what he'd done.

But she was here in his house.

He'd tried so hard to keep her away.

"I'm glad he's not died." The plaintive voice rose up the stairs.

Petey with the matching brown eyes that saw too much for a four-year-old was here, too. Sam shut his eyes.

Rising like heat from the sidewalk, Hannah's low voice floated around him. "C'mon, sugar, we've got to go wash these sheets and blanket as soon as Sam wakes up, and then I have to talk to your preschool teacher about making some kind of permanent arrangements."

"Won't go back there."

"Petey, we don't have any choice. You have to."

"Petey does not like it there. At all."

"Oh, sugar, I wish I could take you with me, but I can't. You know that."

"I would sit very still." Hopeful.

"Of course you would, honey, but we can't do that. I can't drag you around all day on interviews with me. No matter how still you sat, you'd be miserable."

"I am very mizzbul at that school. Nobody likes me. I hate it there. Don't make me go!" Despair and defeat.

"Petey, if there were anything else I could do, I would, you have to believe me. I love you more than anything in the world. You know that, sugar." Despair and defeat in Hannah's voice, too.

Slow and easy, with a slight drawl, her voice was made for dancing cheek to cheek in a smoky, crowded room with the lights low and music curling around your body and through it, moving a man and a woman until both music and bodies blended.

A long time ago in another life, he'd danced like that, close and tight and hungry for what would come later. He'd known that kind of more-than-anything-in-the-world love, too.

Sam closed his ears to Hannah's voice and tried to sit up. He grunted.

Not going to be a good day. Sweat beaded on his forehead. He clamped his teeth together and strained up. Sweat poured down his back and soaked his shirt by the time he finally let his head fall back against the headboard. But he'd made it.

As he listened to the voices, he reminded himself for the millionth time that pushing his body through pain was all he could do.

"Okay, sugar pie, what's the problem? Why such a face? It'll freeze like that, you know."

Breathing deeply, Sam listened, picturing the curious little scene. Without being there, he knew Hannah was kneeling close to Petey, and, judging from the light teasing in Hannah's voice, Petey was making a doozer of a face.

Making a doozer of a face himself, Sam struggled to brace himself so that he could slide out from under the spread.

He didn't have enough control in his shaking legs to keep his feet from thudding onto the floor. Hunched over, pulling in deep breaths to steady himself, Sam gathered his strength for the next effort.

Gritting his teeth, he straightened his arms at the edge of the bed and looked up to two pairs of matching brown eyes peering around the door.

A set of the longest legs he'd ever seen in his life moved into view. "Sam?" Smoke in the wind, Hannah's voice carried her worry to him.

"Yeah. Me." He looked straight into her warm brown eyes and wished for a fleeting moment that the hazy memories had been real. Could be real.

Wished she weren't seeing him like this.

"Are you okay?" Her foot hovered just outside his room.

Petey clutched Hannah's thigh tightly with both chubby arms, his eyes like pie plates.

"Yeah. Sure." Trying to sort out reality from dreams, Sam frowned. "What are you doing here?"

"Uh," she hesitated, her eyebrows drawing together in a thin, satin brown line. "Um."

"Mommy, tell him." Petey pulled at her arm. "We sleeped here," he said importantly to Sam while Hannah fidgeted on both feet.

"Oh." Sam looked at Hannah with her wispy hair sliding heedlessly around her oval face.

Tired eyes underlined with dark circles gazed cautiously back at him.

"Why?" he asked.

Petey opened his mouth to answer, but Hannah raced into speech and stalled. "Well, uh, um."

"Not much of a talker early in the morning, are you?" Sam thought no man alive would mind finding Hannah Randall in his bed early in the morning with her soft hair floating around her sleepy face. Wouldn't much matter at first whether she talked or not. But a man would want that low voice murmuring to him.

"Uh, no." She shifted again, clearly uneasy, and thrust her fingers through the tumult of her hair, sending it tumbling and curling every which way.

"So why'd you sleep in my house?" Sam wanted to stand up, walk over to her, touch that warm mass of bright brown hair and see if it was as soft as it looked. He wouldn't dare. "I don't remember inviting you to a pajama party," he said, letting testiness kill the yearning to touch her.

"No." Hannah paused for a moment, gauging his mood, and then she looked down at Petey, who squirmed beside her. "Why don't you go downstairs for a minute, sugar? I'll be right with you, okay?"

Petey frowned. "No." He wiggled his small butt back and forth. "Wanna stay here." He glanced at the closet. "Wanna find out about my—"

"Peter Robert Randall. Now. Downstairs." Hannah's voice brooked no nonsense.

Sam looked at the boy.

Scowling up at her, Petey propped his fists on his hips. "Not going to go. Don't want to."

Interest dulling his pain, Sam wondered how Hannah would resolve the stalemate. He straightened. Despite her apparent fragility and softness, Hannah had a core of steel. Based on what he'd seen so far, she had an inner strength that kept her going in spite of overwhelming circumstances. But he knew her son was her weakness.

Ignoring Sam, Hannah stooped to Petey's level. She touched his face gently. "I know you want to stay. You can't. I need you to go downstairs now, sugar. We'll talk later, at home." She stood up and wrapped her arm around her son's shoulders. "Go on, Peter Robert. Now." Steel in a velvet glove.

Big brown eyes stared pitifully up at her. Petey's mouth quivered. Hannah shook her head twice. Ducking his head down, Petey gave up. Small footsteps tramped down the hall.

From downstairs, Petey's disgruntled murmurs carried back to them. "I'm all alone and lonesome down here, and I don't like it by myself, and it's not fair, and I am not happy. Petey Robert Randall is not happy."

Hannah shrugged at Sam. "I'm sorry." She crossed her arms around her waist. "You're wondering why I'm in your house."

Sam shrugged and ignored the stab of pain shooting down his spine. "I'm a little curious, yes." Through half-closed eyes, he watched the light move over her face and touch that whiskey brown hair with gold. He wanted to touch her hair more than he'd wanted to do anything in a long time, and that scared him. He balled up his fists in the spread.

Staying at the door, Hannah asked, "Do you remember me giving you your medicine last night?"

Sam nodded. That part was clear.

"I left to check on Petey. I came back."

Looking out the window down onto her car, Sam wished for a fleeting second he'd never made that phone call that had involved himself in Hannah's life. He'd opened a door he couldn't close. "When? I don't remember much of anything after I took my pill."

"You were almost asleep." She stepped forward, hesitating. "The medicine seemed to make you confused." Indecisive, she edged toward him. "You'd managed to get to your room. I was worried that you'd hurt yourself."

Sam knew she was leaving something out, and he stirred up the pond of his memories. A glimpse of her face over his, her small body sprawled soft and warm across him. The image floated to the top like a leaf swirling in darkness, and his body flushed.

He glanced at her, his eyes narrowing in thought.

Hannah avoided his eyes, but her face was pink.

It was true then. He had kissed her. Had pulled her down beside him and wanted to keep her there. He remembered the piercing hunger now, the way he'd wanted to forget everything and take her with him into oblivion. "I see." He looked away.

"Anyway, I can see now that you're fine, so Petey—" she began.

"I told you to run. Far and fast." His fingers clenched in the spread as he remembered that hopeless hunger.

"You did."

He could barely hear her. The slide of her hands over her arms and her slight inhalation of breath reminded him of the way she'd felt under his hands, reminded him of the quiet sound she'd made as he kissed her. "Why didn't you stay away?"

She went still.

Downstairs Petey's grumbles blurred into a monotone. Sam waited.

Finally Hannah answered. "I was afraid you might need something during the night."

Sam looked at her then, looked at the soft mouth he remembered taking with a hunger beyond anything he'd known. "You shouldn't have come back, Hannah Randall." A vague sense of soft fingers moving over his aching body again and again, bringing ease, flashed in his mind. "It was a mistake."

Something must have shown in his face because suddenly Hannah was backing out the door and talking fast. Her legs gleamed in a sudden patch of bright sunshine. "Petey and I slept downstairs. We're leaving now. We won't be a problem. I just wanted to make sure you were okay before we left, that's all. Really, we're not going to make pests of ourselves."

She was in the hall.

"Hannah." The rough edge of his voice startled him and caused Hannah to stumble. Sam didn't even know what he wanted to say, knew he was a fool to keep her near him one second longer than he had to, but he couldn't help himself, and the words came out strangled and harsh through his tight lips. "Hannah, wait. Please."

She stopped.

He saw the slight trembling in her body and wondered what else had happened that she wasn't telling him and he couldn't remember. "I have to thank you."

"No, not at all. I didn't do anything. Really. Medicine can disorient people, that's all, and you're here alone. I was worried that you'd be confused in the night. I just stayed to make sure you were okay, but you slept through the night. I never heard a sound."

She still wouldn't look him in the eyes. His medication always knocked him out. He would have been helpless, the way he dreaded. Suddenly Sam understood that she was trying to protect him, and he hated it. "I don't need a baby-sitter. I don't want you taking care of me."

He wanted to stride over to her, take her narrow shoulders up in his hands and show her he didn't need her help.

He couldn't.

For the first time since the accident, anger at his own helplessness bathed Sam. This new anger thundered over his knowledge that he deserved every one of his injuries and dragged him upright.

Her face crinkled with worry, Hannah stretched out a hand to him. "Are you okay?"

"Do you see yourself as the world's caretaker?" he ground out through pain. "I live here alone by choice. Whatever happens to me is my problem, not yours! If I wanted someone hovering around me, I'd hire a nanny, so if I fall over on the sidewalk, just walk on by, hear?" Clinging to the wall, he spit out the words.

Instead, she stared at him. Her hand dropped to her side, and then, as he glared at her, a smile moved in her eyes.

"Walk right by?" That mischievous smile worked into the corners of her mouth and tucked the soft edges into dimples. "I suppose you want me to give you a friendly little kick, too?"

Watching the sweetness and understanding in her eyes, Sam felt the anger seep out of him. "I'm acting like a fool, huh?"

She nodded, and her hair trailed around her, catching sunlight and his eyes. "A little. Maybe acting more like a four-year-old."

"Like Petey, right?"

"Worse." She smiled at him.

"You don't back off, do you?" He liked that.

"No. I'm nobody's doormat." Her face tightened and then softened as she grinned at him. "Besides, you can't survive a four-year-old if you're a marshmallow."

"I reckon not," Sam said. "I wouldn't know." He thought only about Petey. "He's a nice kid."

"Most of the time," she said in a sweet voice that said she'd love the kid even if he were rotten most of the time. "Anyway, I imagine you really pushed yourself yesterday. Are you sore this morning?"

"Sorehead, I reckon." He leaned on the wall and, using it for support, dropped slowly and gratefully back onto the bed. "Yeah, I feel as though I've been trampled by a herd of bulls, but other than that, not bad." Sam looked down at her feet rather than face her.

One pink toe poked through the hole of one raggedy sneaker.

Everything was spinning out of his control, and he didn't know why. The blissful numbness that had protected him for so long had evaporated in the heat of anger. No, earlier, when curiosity about Hannah and her son had prickled though him like needles. All the feelings he'd thought were dead were tumbling him around on a roller-coaster ride of emotions, and he didn't know where or when the ride was going to pitch him off.

"Can I get you anything before Petey and I leave, or are you going to bite my head off for offering?" The small pink toe rubbed the heel of the other raggedy sneaker.

Sam looked away from the wiggly toe that made him wonder what the rest of her narrow foot looked like. "Maybe a padlock for my mouth so I'll have half a chance to think before I spout off?"

"Sounds like a promising idea. I'll let you know if I find one big enough." She glanced sideways at him, and a teasing smile crept over her face.

Sam liked that smile. Hannah Randall had a hell of a terrific smile. Like sunshine behind a cloud. A little tentative at first, peeping out, then shining wide and warm and wonderful. A million-dollar smile. It made him want to surprise it out of hiding and keep it shining on him until it filled up all the cold darkness inside him. "Do that."

"Well, bye. You take care, now, hear?"

Sam couldn't let her go just yet. "I wish you hadn't come back last night." He meant it, but wondered why the words felt like a lie.

"Well, I did, so let's forget it, all right?" She tilted her head, listening downstairs. "You helped me, so we're even, right?" Her words carried a slight challenge.

Sam knew she was talking about the tow truck again. She wouldn't give up. "Don't know what you mean," he said, perversity ruling him and making him keep her off balance. He liked the way her mouth pursed as she frowned at his answer.

Watching him closely, she shrugged again and made a mocking face. "Right. Sure." Turning to leave, she hesitated, that million-dollar smile flashing at him over her shoulder and flooding him with warmth. "If you're truly in the dark about my red-haired angel of mercy, I figure I still owe you, Sam Dennehy, and I always pay my debts."

"You don't owe me anything, Hannah." Sam shaded his eyes, not wanting her to leave.

"Have it your way, then." She paused and then, in a butter-wouldn't-melt-on-toast voice, added, "But tell your friend I'm not the cookie-baby type, will you?'' She wrinkled up her nose and slipped out the door.

Letting his hand drop, watching her slim figure disappear out of his sight after all, for a moment Sam felt as though all the sunlight in the room had flowed after her down the dark staircase.

In the silence after Hannah and her son left, loneliness ached inside Sam, warring with the ache of his body. He leaned back against the headboard, wondering for the first time in a very long time what he was going to do with the rest of his worthless, unwanted life now that he'd returned from the living dead.

He didn't thank Hannah Randall and her big-eyed son for dragging him into the sunlight.

Chapter Five

Back in her house as she stuffed the washing machine with Sam's sheets and blanket, Hannah tried to harden her heart to Petey's laments. All morning long, mumbling through his peanut-butter toast and milk breakfast, trailing her like a sad shadow, eyes big and pleading, hoping against hope, Petey had begged her.

"They tease me, Mommy." He pulled at the edge of her shirt.

"Oh, Petey." She piled the dry towels on top of the washing machine and began to fold. "Here, Petey, you get the washcloths." She tossed him a confetti-colored heap. "Who teases you?"

"Ev'rybody." He painstakingly lined up the edges of a pink cloth. "They make fun of me. I will not go back, you know." His square face was filled with determination, and tears clung to the corners of his eyes.

Her helplessness to protect her son ripped through her like a knife. "Why would anybody do that?" Holding a folded towel tightly to her chest Hannah sank onto the floor. She was just about ready to throw in the towel. Literally, she added, with an edgy flash of still-surviving humor.

Dropping his pile of laundry and plodding over to her, Petey got on his knees and took her face between his hands, making her look at him. His nose bumped hers as he whispered tearfully, "I can't tell you. Just please don't make me go back, Mommy."

"You have to tell me, sugar." Hannah placed her hands on top of his. "We don't keep secrets, remember? Secrets can hurt. We'll fix whatever is wrong."

His tear-wet eyelashes sparkled in front of her. He sniffed drippily and leaned his forehead against hers. "Can't be fixed," he sighed.

"Listen, sugar, Mommy will make it all right. I *promise,*" Hannah spoke rashly in her urgency to find out what was bothering Petey.

"Can't. Even a mommy can't fix this." He licked the tears off his upper lip.

Hannah was so tired she could sit right down and bawl with him. What if there were something even worse than what she was already hearing? Children were so vulnerable. She counted to five and plunged on. "Tell me anyway, honey. I'll do the best I can. Okay?" She lifted his face and looked at him. "What happened, Petey?"

A deep sigh came from the region of Petey's baby-soft tummy. "They laugh at me when I run. I trip on my foot and fall down."

"Oh." Hannah understood everything now. Petey was right. Not even a mommy could fix what was happening in Petey's life. She wrapped her arms tightly around him and rocked silently back and forth, giving Petey the comfort she wished someone could give her.

"I don't let 'em see me cry. I hide."

"Don't the teachers see what's happening?"

"Prob'ly not." He wound his stubby finger in the strands of hair hanging around her face.

She'd make them watch out for her son. She'd make them see they had to stop the playground cruelty at least, but she knew with the awful fatalism of adulthood that her efforts would only be a Band-Aid. She couldn't protect Petey from this kind of playground meanness. "Where are the teachers when all this teasing happend?"

"Around," Petey said, and untwined his finger. "I am not a tattletale, Mommy," he finished. "You won't make me go back now I told you, will you?"

Looking at his expectant face, Hannah would have given everything in her power to say no and protect Petey from life's harshness, but he was going to have to face what would happen and deal with it. Even at four, he was going to have to find that strength somewhere in his small heart. Her heart ached for him. "Listen to me, sugar. I don't want to send you back there. That's one truth."

"Good," he said, and started to wiggle off her lap, happiness restored by mommy magic.

"But," Hannah continued slowly, her heart full and hurting with her helplessness, "the second truth is—"

Petey turned and put both hands over her mouth. "Don't want to hear 'nother truth. First one is okeydokey." His eyebrows quirked up. "Don't tell me no more. Okay?"

Very gently Hannah removed his hands and held them, remembering another truth she'd had to tell him, how it had torn her apart to face him with the facts of the divorce. "Petey, I can do a lot of things, but you were right. I can't fix this. I don't have anywhere else for you to go. I have to find a job. You have to go to the center."

"No!"

Hannah swallowed the lump in her throat and held him close to her. Making Petey face his tormentors was almost worse than telling him about the divorce. At least then she'd been able to reassure him that she'd be with him. She couldn't do that now.

"No!" he sobbed while she stared blindly out the window at the bright tropical day.

"There's nothing Mommy can do, sugar." Hannah rubbed his back, up and down, cuddling him. "Please believe me. I need your help, Petey. You have to be a very big, very brave boy and go back. Just for a while." She smoothed his hair as he looked up at her.

Hopelessness stared back at her from Petey's eyes, cutting her to the quick.

If she'd been able, she would have spared Petey the knowledge that grown-ups were sometimes powerless, too. "Can you do that for Mommy?"

Warm sunlight pooled around her, but she was cold and lonely inside, helpless and scared. Kids needed two parents, she thought bleakly. She was all Petey had, and she wasn't doing a real bang-up job.

She took a quavery breath. She'd just have to go on doing the best she could. That was how life worked. You kept doing whatever you had to do. And maybe saying a small prayer or two in the dark night hours when fear whipped close against you.

Hannah stood up, hanging on to Petey with one arm and grabbing towels with the other. "C'mon, sugar, let's splurge and have a peppermint ice cream cone, what do you say?"

"Okeydoke," Petey replied with no enthusiasm, and tucked his head under her chin. "But my dragon, *he'd* fix things, I betcha."

"Petey, *please,* don't start about the dragon again, sugar. We have to face what's ahead of us and not pretend so much, hear?" Hannah didn't think she had an ounce of energy left to deal with Petey's imaginary dragon stories. She was having enough trouble dealing with reality.

Petey wouldn't look at her as he mumbled something under his breath. She could just about wish for a dragon of her own right now, Hannah thought as she gulped back her own tears, but she held on to Petey and concentrated on getting both of them upright and out to the car.

Peppermint ice cream wasn't a magic dragon, but it was real and cold on a ninety-eight-degree day with matching humidity, and she could afford two double dippers. *That* was a reality she could control.

Later she'd figure out some way of handling everything else. Maybe. Prob'ly, as Petey would say.

But the phone rang as they were heading out the door, and an interview at one of the elementary schools in her neighborhood had opened, and so, as she dressed and hurried a too-quiet Petey out the door to the preschool day-care center, once again Hannah felt life spinning her along in its own current, sweeping away all her hard-earned efforts.

Later, in the afternoon heat with her just-ironed blouse limp, the job only a remote possibility and Petey still silent and withdrawn, Hannah wondered how much longer she could keep up the juggling act. Sooner or later everything was going to come crashing around her ears.

Deliberately she slowed her breathing and lifted the cans of fruit and soup out of the cabinet, forcing herself to focus on what she could touch and see in a compelling need to keep her terror at bay. The bright labels were real. The can opener was real. Jell-O was real. And wobbly. Like her.

"I'm going outside," Petey finally said after wandering silently in and out of the kitchen, upstairs and down, his lonely footsteps striking nails into her heart.

"Okay. I'll call you when supper's ready." Hannah hugged him and let him wander out to the yard. He didn't feel like talking, and she didn't, either.

Scuffling in the grass, Petey kicked up a grasshopper and watched it fly toward the deeper grass at the back of the yard. Trailing its green buzz, Petey followed it to the fence where the twilight shadows had already fallen.

Everything next door was quiet.

He'd liked sleeping at Mr. Sam's, but he wished he'd seen where the dragon slept. Maybe the dragon had flown away, like the grasshopper. Prob'ly. That's how life was lately.

Crawling up on the tree stump, Petey leaned against the fence and pressed the Band-Aid on his knee. He'd been shoved off the bench into the shells on the playground, but he hadn't cried even though he'd wanted to. Lifting up the Band-Aid, he poked at the red skin. Not as bad as Mr. Sam's knees.

For a while he dozed, his face pressed against the old wood as night moved into the garden.

The smell of smoke and the sound of creaking woke him up. His heart pounded as he put his eye to the hole and saw the dull red eye.

The dragon hadn't flown away!

"Hey, there, it's me again," Petey whispered, afraid to speak louder and scare away the dragon. "Where you been?"

"Around," the dragon muttered.

"I don't never see you during the day."

"I sleep a lot."

"Oh. I don't like to go to bed."

"There wasn't anything to wake up for. Until you came."

Petey breathed deeply. The dragon had come awake just for him. Just because he needed him.

There was a long silence while the red eye moved in the dark, and then the dragon's scratchy voice answered. "Hey, Petey. How was your day?"

"Bad." Petey sighed. "How 'bout yours?" he asked politely, remembering his manners.

"Not so good." The dragon's sigh was a deeper echo of Petey's.

"I'm real sorry."

"Well, that's how things go some days."

"I know," Petey said forlornly, remembering how he'd felt when he lay on the shells and everybody was laughing. "Life is very tough sometimes for a four-year-old."

The red eye burned brighter, and the dragon gave a small chuckle. "Yeah, kid, it sure can be. Even for grown-ups."

"Even for you, huh?"

There was a long silence, and Petey was afraid he'd been rude and the dragon was gone, but finally the answer came low and raspy. "Yeah."

Petey sat quietly and pulled off the Band-Aid while he thought. Finally he said, "Bad day for Mommy, too."

"Oh?" A different shade of interest in the dragon's rough voice.

"Yeah," Petey answered. "I thought she could do any-thing, but she couldn't change the bad stuff at school for me, and she was sad."

"I would have been sad, too," the dragon added, and desolation colored his raspy tones.

"But you can do anything. There ain't nothin' you can't do."

The dragon stirred. "I wish that were true. More than you know, I wish I could change a lot of things."

"Like what?" Petey watched the dark bulk of the dragon shift slightly and heard his muffled sigh.

"Too many things to name." The dragon shifted. "What would you change, Petey Randall?"

"No more preschool center," Petey said breathlessly. "I hate it, hate it, and I tried so hard to be brave for Mommy, but I couldn't. I'm only four years old and not very brave. Mommy thinks I am, but I stood it and I cannot take it anymore," he wound up, trying to keep the dragon from hearing the sobs shaking his chest. "Alfred makes all the other kids call me a *doofus* and nobody lets me be on their team. I am not a *doofus!*"

Petey shoved his T-shirt in his mouth to quiet his wails.

The dragon's red eye grew brighter. "Tell me about it, Petey."

And Petey did, filling the air with his lonely misery while his dragon listened patiently until the last syllables died away in the night.

"That's a lot to face." The dragon shifted carefully. "I don't think I could have been as brave as you were."

"But what am I going to do now? Mommy done all she could, and I still have to go back. Until Mommy gets a job." And then, like the flickering light on the fireflies, an idea and hope blinked in Petey. He sat up straight on the stump. "But *you* could do something!"

"I don't think so," the dragon said slowly, his red eye moving in the dark.

"I know you can! You fixed things before!" Off in the distance, Petey heard his mommy calling for him to come in.

"Supper, sugar! Come on in."

"Please! You can do anything! Will you?" he asked urgently, slipping off the stump. "You can fix ev'rything all better!"

"Wait!" rushed the dragon's voice after him, but Petey had gone.

Hannah caught him belting into the house, his Petey-grin spread wide across his face. She caught him to her and felt her heart ease its pain a little at the sparkle in his eyes.

"I talked to my dragon. Gonna be okeydokey," he said importantly as he dragged a chair to the table. "I ain't gonna haf' to go back to that ol' school." Over the purple rim of the plastic milk glass, his bright brown eyes watched her.

"Petey, I told you how things were," Hannah said, pulling up her own chair and searching deep inside her for some way to help Petey see that there were no miracles on the horizon for them.

"Me and you don't gotta worry no more, Mommy, b'lieve me." Petey slid the fruit Jell-O over to her and drained his cup of soup noisily.

Hannah watched the lime green shimmer and shake in the light and lowered her head to the table.

Petey patted her cheek.

Sam sat in the darkness and watched the light and movement in Hannah's house. Drawn to the light like a self-destructive moth, he thought. Leaning his head back, he looked up at the heavens. He would be stupid to involve himself more deeply in Hannah's life. In Petey's.

The misery in the childish voice lingered in the air while Sam stared at the moon beginning to rise over the horizon.

Too much unhappiness in the world.

Nothing he could do to change life.

"Hannah Randall!" The voice came from nowhere, everywhere in the dark.

Gripping Petey tight against her as they sat on the back porch steps after supper, Hannah looked down the alleyway and couldn't believe her eyes. Even with the porch light off, she recognized the figure slowly moving toward her.

The man shouldn't have been able to get out of bed. How he could be hobbling toward her, propped up on crutches, was beyond Hannah's wildest imaginings. Slumped over the supports, face twisted and pale with the effort he was making, he finally stopped and stood, looking at her with those guarded eyes.

Unable to believe what she saw, she focused on the reality of the crutches. "Where's your wheelchair?"

He ignored her question and plodded grimly toward her.

How could he possibly be mobile? "*What* are you doing in my backyard?" she managed to get out.

"I want to talk to you." He edged forward gingerly. "And Petey."

Hannah could feel the blood draining right out of her head as he looked at her. Shaky and confused, she stared at Sam Dennehy's angular, square-chinned, determined face.

Bewildered didn't even begin to describe how she felt, she thought as she stood up, swaying on her feet, light-headed.

"Will you come here?" His mouth moved in what tried to be a smile as he indicated the grass. "I don't think I can make it much farther. If I did get up your stairs, the only way you'd get me back home is if you slapped my heels behind my ears and bounced me down, maybe, like a big rubber ball."

Intrigued by the picture Sam described, Petey straightened in Hannah's arms, and she almost dropped him.

Sam sank to the grass. He leaned the crutches against the bottom step. "Can I talk to you? For a minute or two?"

In a trance, mesmerized by the will flashing in his hazel eyes, Hannah found herself placing one foot in front of the other until she was standing above Sam. He'd braced his right foot on the lower step, and his arm stretched out behind him, a light shadow against the dark grass.

She started to step back, but he reached up and his firm grip stopped her. "No. Stay."

A faint tremor ran from his long fingers to her elbow. She looked at his lean hand closed around her arm. His thumb and little finger made a loose circle just above the bend. His thumb moved against the sensitive skin of her inner arm.

There was such strength in his one hand that she suddenly, irrationally, longed to fling herself on his wide chest and rest there, his powerful shoulders a harbor from the storm her life had become.

Petey slid down her side and bumped to the ground. "Hey, there, Mr. Sam. I like your TV."

"You do?" Sam moved his thumb once, and Hannah felt the slide of skin on skin in the pit of her stomach, warming her where she'd been cold and frightened.

Petey nodded energetically.

Hannah gathered herself together. How easily Sam had distracted Petey.

"How about my yard? Do you like that, too?"

Cocking his head, Petey looked puzzled. "'Course."

"Good." Satisfaction rippled in Sam's voice, and he glanced at Hannah.

Like crystals in sunlight, the hazel of his eyes shifted from brown to light green and back, lightening as he looked at her. In their depths was a strange, unsettling expression, and for a moment Hannah felt as though she were under some curious spell where only that shifting light in his eyes kept her upright.

She started to speak and found words had fled her mind. He tugged gently on her arm, and she slumped onto the grass. As she dropped, her leg slid past Sam's, and the soft hairs of his thigh brushed her knee. Her kneecap tingled, prickled. As he watched her, the centers of his eyes darkened and her blood beat thick and heavy and slow in the silence.

The night wind, soft and warm, slipped along her skin, and she was caught in his gaze while the air glided, touching, lifting her hair, and his eyes followed each touch of the breeze on her.

Her toes curled.

Sam's hair was rumpled and his chin whisker-shaded, but he had an expression on his face she hadn't seen. He wanted something, and in his own way he looked as determined as Petey had earlier.

With a big difference. Petey was a child. Sam Dennehy wasn't.

From his wide shoulders and muscled arms to the long legs stretched beside her, he was every inch a man, and the determination gleaming in his eyes was that of a man who clearly could make himself do anything he wanted to.

A man outside her experience.

Held in thrall, Hannah nevertheless began to wonder what curveball life was about to pitch her way. She knew she couldn't handle anything new. The scenes with Petey had left her empty and drained.

His hand still circling her arm, Sam said, "I won't be polite and pretend I didn't hear what you and your son were talking about." He looked at Petey, who'd plopped down on the bottom step and was playing with the rubber tips of the crutches. "This is about Petey. And me." He cleared his throat.

"Go on," Hannah said from her faraway place where anything seemed possible. Probable. Petey's dragon could come lumbering out of the dark, and she wouldn't even blink.

"You know I hated having you see me the way I was last night." He cleared his throat again and looked away for a brief second before looking back at her and taking her breath away again with his intense stare.

Hannah nodded.

"Some days I don't go downstairs at all. Not even to eat."

Again Hannah nodded.

"My days are long." He ran his free hand over his hair. With a life of its own, it sprang right back up, alive and shining. "Lonely." The admission was reluctantly offered.

As if lifted against her will, Hannah's fingers reached out to smooth flat the brown strands shining in the dark. Her hand lingered in the air and then dropped to her side as he continued.

"Petey doesn't want to go back to his day-care center."

"Preschool," Hannah corrected in a daze. "Though it's not a real difference, I suppose."

"Whatever the place is, I know Petey isn't happy there."

Standing up, Petey declared, "I am not." He stepped down one stair and back up, over and over, saying, "Am not, am not. So there."

"I heard you talking downstairs this morning." Sam laid his palm over Petey's head. "That's what I want to talk to your mom about. Will you sit for a sec while I ask her for a favor?"

"Yep." Petey folded himself up beside Hannah.

Sam Dennehy wouldn't ask her for a favor. He'd made that abundantly clear. She understood, too. She didn't blame him. In fact, she admired his prickly independence even while she wanted to swat him for being so stupid about it. He was up to something, and lost in exhaustion she couldn't stay a step ahead of him. Her words were thready as she said, "A favor? I find that hard to swallow."

"Sort of a favor, then." He leaned forward, and she felt as though she were on top of a tall building, irresistibly drawn to the sheer edge. "I have a proposition for you. A trade-off, if you'll agree."

"What?"

"My days are long, Petey's are miserable—I think that was the word he used." Sam tightened the grip he'd maintained. "Let Petey stay at my house. With me."

"No. Absolutely not." Energy coursed through Hannah, freeing her at last from the spell of Sam's gaze.

"Mommy!" Petey wailed, standing up and glaring at her. "You're messing it all up! I told you it was gonna be okey-dokey, and you're gonna ruin it!"

Before Hannah could stop him, he ran out into the deeper shadows to the back of the yard.

Struggling to her feet, she started to go after him, but once more Sam's grasp halted her.

"Hannah," he said, "listen to the rest of what I have to say before you decide, fair enough?"

"I don't think I want to. You play dirty, Sam Dennehy." Hannah glared at him and then frowned as she realized she was duplicating Petey's indignant expression.

"Dirty pool?"

She nodded emphatically.

"Because I brought it up in front of Petey?"

"Yes! That wasn't fair. Or nice."

"I agree."

"You do?" Amazed, she sank back down. "Then why did you do it? Why bring up such an outlandish idea while he was listening?"

"Because I didn't think it through."

"That's a lousy line of reasoning. What kind of behavior is that? To use my child against me in order to get what you want?"

"Damned inexcusable, rotten, abominable behavior? I know it was. What can I say?" He grimaced.

Hannah checked herself in midsentence. "Oh."

"I know how important your son is to you. Since the situation involved him, too, I wanted him to hear the idea. I wish now I'd come at you differently."

"You should have figured out a way."

"Right. I hit you on your blind side. I know that. Freely admit I was out of line. I didn't know how else to get you to listen. I'm not very good at subtlety, more like a bull in a china shop, I reckon."

"I don't understand."

"I've lost the knack of talking to people." He shrugged and looked away from her. "The idea kind of popped in my head, and I came over."

"Oh," she responded, somewhat stunned.

"Could we still talk about my idea? The idea's good even if I went about bringing it up all wrong." He smiled, a slight movement of his mouth.

That smile, though not much more than an upward tilting of his lips, was so real and surprising, so self-mocking, that Hannah found her anger leaving her in the face of his admission. "I'm probably out of my mind, but why not? Go ahead." She ran her hands through her hair, pulling with both fists in the hope that the small tweaks would bring her to her clearly abandoned senses.

"Why is it an outlandish idea?" Sam leaned back from her and bolstered himself against the step.

Thinking, Hannah squinted. "You don't take favors. That's one reason. Another is that I can't see how having Petey underfoot would be to *your* benefit."

He didn't answer.

"You're not used to having a small boy around all day. Petey can be a handful. And—" Hannah wasn't too sure how much she wanted to tell this stranger who didn't seem like one anymore but still was, so she stopped, at a loss. Finally she added, "He's having some problems lately. He wouldn't stay with you."

"What if he agreed to? He hates what he's doing now, but he's been toughing it out. Why not ask him if he'd rather stay with me? Why not let him decide?"

"No! You're rushing me!" Panic fluttered through her. She'd known Sam Dennehy, even in a wheelchair and on crutches, had power to burn, and now, with all that force directed toward her, she wanted to run.

"I don't mean to push."

"Well, you are. And I think you mean to." Hannah knew she sounded petulant, ungrateful, but she'd run through the last of her reserves some time earlier in the day. "You're crowding me," she whispered, feeling the strength of that indomitable will pulsing against her even though he wasn't touching her. She had nothing left with which to defend herself against a Sam committed to a course of action she found unacceptable.

Unacceptable because it was so tempting. Unbearably tempting to surrender to the force of his will and let him solve her problems. And ultimately his idea was unacceptable because it *would* solve those problems. She'd worked too hard for her independence to yield it so easily and put her in his debt when she had no way of repaying him.

He leaned forward and gripped his knees. The crutches bumped onto the ground as his foot dislodged them. "I'm sorry. Let me back up, see if I can do this better, okay?"

She lowered her head to avoid his eyes, but his harsh voice breathed around her.

"I know this is personal, and I'm sorry for prying, but I reckon you'd take Petey out of the school if you could afford to, right?"

She nodded, not looking up, just resting her head on her knees.

"But you're paying something now, aren't you? The school isn't free, is it?"

"No," she whispered, exhausted.

"So how can you afford to send him? Even there?"

Hannah dragged her head up on a neck that wasn't strong enough to support it. Her head drooped back to her knees as she murmured, "I work a couple of afternoons a week there to pay Petey's expenses. That's the only way I can afford someone to look after him while I look for a full-time job. Without that arrangement, I don't know what I'd do."

"What about an arrangement with me?"

Something stirred in Sam's voice that brought Hannah's head snapping up. "What do you mean?"

Leaning so close to her that his face filled her field of vision, he said in a voice that rubbed against the quiet night sounds, "You know I don't get out?"

"Yes?" Hannah stared at him.

"You saw my refrigerator?" Rough, glittering with the energy he was directing her way, the words darted toward her.

"I did." A slow humming ran along her skin, and her exhaustion fled before the electricity coursing through her, coming from him to her.

"I haven't been interested in food, not interested in much of anything for a long time. I thought maybe you might trade off making my evening meals. Or lunches. I wouldn't care. I can't cook." He sighed and gripped his knees tighter.

"Can't? Or don't?"

"Does it matter?"

Hannah thought. "Yes, to me it does."

"All right." He nodded, understanding. "I can cook. I don't."

"Are you offering charity, then?" She had to know. Her skin buzzed faster as his gaze enclosed her.

"No."

"A meal every night doesn't seem like an even trade. What's in this arrangement for you?"

"I don't know. But it's important to me. I do know that, and I'm being honest with you. I'm not offering charity."

Hannah studied him, not understanding anything at all except that a miracle lay within her grasp, and all she had to do was reach out and seize it. "Why would you want to disrupt your life this way? What's my son to you?"

"Only an unhappy little boy. And I can make him less unhappy for a while." His face was in shadow now, and she couldn't see his expression, but the temptation of all he was offering hung between them in the summer night like the shining star on top of a Christmas tree.

"I don't even know you!" she said.

"Yes, you do. You know everything essential about me, Hannah, just as I know you." He touched her cheek. "Willy-nilly, we're neighbors. That's a start."

"But—"

"Anything else you want to know, ask. I'll answer your questions. I'll give you character references. Ask, Hannah, that's all you have to do. So easy."

The back of his finger slid to her chin, leaving warmth and comfort in its wake. His hand clasped his knee again, and the breeze was cool on her skin where he'd touched her. Hannah pressed her fists to her face. Could she? Could it be this simple?

"Ask Petey. Can't you swallow your pride enough to see how right this would be? For Petey? For me? For you, too,

Hannah Randall," he said, and the shifting light in his intense eyes drew her in to the possibility.

"I don't know," she whispered while the night stirred around her and hinted of impossible things made real. "Maybe I'm babying him. Maybe he needs to face this situation and deal with it."

"He *is* a baby. He's *been* handling that mess with the other kids, and he's reached his limit, don't you think? For a little guy?"

His voice rode with the breeze, saying out loud what she believed in the deepest part of her heart.

"Come on, Hannah. Make it easy on yourself. Ask Petey," Sam's hoarse voice urged, seducing her with hope, carrying away her will to resist.

Chapter Six

"It will work," said Sam. "Watch." Pulling his crutches to him, he stood up, and even in the uncertain light, Hannah saw his knuckles bleach out on the crutch supports. "Petey!"

The small shadow swooping down on them would have knocked Hannah down, but Sam snagged him, somehow balancing them both until Hannah lifted Petey up in her arms, making a sandwich of him between her and Sam.

"Yep?"

"Petey, your mom—"

"Sugar—"

"I told you it would be all right, Mommy."

The voices overlapped and words collided against each other.

Carrying Petey to the porch step, Hannah settled him on her lap.

Sam's breath was a warm puff of air against her bare knees as he eased himself down on the step below her. Over his right shoulder, the rising moon silvered its way into the summer night.

It hung there, out of her reach, but so close and bright Hannah had the strangest feeling she could pluck it right out of the air if she leaned against Sam's broad shoulders and stretched out her fingers.

The night went still, and in that curious silence, cool silver filled her palms to overflowing, and the hard planes of Sam's chest lay against the curves of her breasts.

Everything, everything out there in the still moment, shining and waiting, waiting for her to seize it, take it, if she only dared reach out.

Looking at Sam's haggard face against the silver crescent, seeing his loneliness, something quivered deep inside her.

And then Petey stirred restlessly, a car backfired and Sam shifted, blocking the moon.

Hannah straightened Petey's shirt, pulling it down over his bare tummy. "Sugar, Sam has a suggestion I want you to listen to. Afterwards tell me what you think, okay?"

"Yep."

Unlike most adults, Sam didn't reach out for Petey in an effort to be chummy with him. Instead, he leaned back and fiddled with his crutch as he spoke. "I have a big, empty yard."

"Yep." Petey made a mustache of a strand of Hannah's hair.

"Nobody uses it all day long. Would you like to share it with me? Instead of going to nursery school?"

"Yep."

Watching Petey's smile spread like syrup over his face, Hannah discovered that pride wasn't all that hard to chew. And, once chewed, it slid down easily enough without the bitter aftertaste she'd expected.

"See how easy, Hannah?"

Gentle mockery underlay Sam's words, and Hannah wanted to tell him that nothing could be as simple as he was making it seem, but there was so much expectancy in Petey's eyes, so much satisfaction in Sam's expression as he glanced from Petey to her, that she only nodded. "Easy," she said, and hoped time would keep that statement true.

Then, as his smile moved into his eyes, she found herself smiling back, lightness and, yes, easiness moving around in her, filling her until she felt as though she might rise up into the warm night like the bright moon.

"Now what?" Sam asked as he stiffly pushed himself to his feet. "When do we start our trade?"

"I'll take those references you mentioned," she said, and prayed he would have them.

"I understand. No problem. Check all you need."

Hannah's breath was shakier than she would have liked. "You have them?"

"Yes." His mouth quirked a little. "And I brush my teeth at least twice a day."

Giving a little bounce on her toes, Hannah shot her final arrow. "I'll bet your dentist is proud of you, but I need a baby-sitter, not a horse."

"Not a baby, Mommy." Petey popped up beside her.

"Anyway," Hannah said, "I'll give you one last chance to change your mind, Sam Dennehy. Fair's fair, and I still don't believe you know what you're getting into."

"Probably not." His teeth flashed in a quick smile as he watched Petey whirling himself dizzily around the yard. "But we have a done deal, Hannah Randall."

Hannah felt her own smile becoming a silly grin in the moonlight and didn't care.

The load she'd shouldered by herself for so long seemed suddenly weightless, and Sam Dennehy was the reason.

Because of him, her son wouldn't have to undergo the daily running of the childish knives. Because of Sam, she wouldn't be torn to bits with the agony of her inability to protect Petey.

Standing hunched over in front of her, his scarred legs needing support, Sam was the most magnificent man she'd ever seen.

"Done." Unable to contain herself, she bounced. "What do you want for dinner tomorrow night, Sam Dennehy?"

"You know something?" Surprise rippled through his voice. "Fried chicken. I think I'd like fried chicken. I can't remember the last time I had any." He frowned.

"Easy!" Calculating quickly that she could afford a chicken if she could get one more wearing out of the nylons she'd run yesterday, Hannah snapped her fingers.

Sam narrowed his eyes on hers, but he didn't say anything. He'd seen the quick glaze pass over her eyes and figured out she was adding up her money. He knew she wouldn't let him pay for the food. If he offered, she'd skin him alive, and he sure didn't know how she was going to manage. He'd have to do some more thinking about the mechanics of this trade-off. He didn't intend for her to do without stuff just to feed him.

Looking down at Petey circling around Hannah's long legs, Sam began to wonder what he was going to do with an energetic four-year-old. Not play tag, that was for damned sure.

Something. He'd have to think about that, too.

"What time will you bring Petey?" Sam was hoping it would be in the afternoon. That would give him time to loosen up. Mornings weren't all that hot.

"Tomorrow, after lunch?" she asked hesitantly.

"Fine."

"Oh, good!"

She smiled that million-dollar smile at him, and Sam forgot to think about his mornings in the sheer pleasure of watching Hannah's silky long legs as she bounced up and down on her toes. Runner's legs. He'd been a runner, too. Sam took a breath. "See you tomorrow, then. I'll have a reference list ready." Wanting to stay, he turned to leave.

"Whoops, careful, sugar." Hannah almost tripped over Petey.

Sam reached out a hand to steady her. His palm slid around her waist, and he grabbed a fistful of her shirt, holding her up as he rocked on his crutches. "Whoa." He could feel her ribs against his hand. Small and delicate, they moved with her laugh.

"See? I told you you didn't know what you were getting into!"

Her face was a clear oval beneath his, brown eyes filled with moonlight and laughing up at him, her slight hips bumping him gently as Petey, tangled between them, tried to free himself. She swayed again, and Sam gathered the thin cotton tighter, holding on as the satin-smooth skin of her back slid underneath his fingers.

Her mouth softened as she looked at him, and Sam remembered how she'd kissed him back, that pink mouth hesitant and then growing warm and full against his.

Holding on to her shirt for dear life, wanting nothing in the world at that moment except to wind her shirt tighter between his fingers until she came as close to him as clothes and skin allowed, Sam remembered after all the last time he'd had fried chicken, remembered other eyes, big and blue, laughing at him, and wanted to turn and run while he still had time.

And couldn't.

He steadied Hannah and twisted his fingers free of her shirt. "Hang on a minute." The metal band of his watch had snagged in her hair as he lifted his hand.

"Sure. I'm not going anywhere." Hannah laughed and reached up to help.

Her laugh was low and musical and vibrated against places in him he'd deadened. "Let me," Sam said, pulling gently, despairingly, at a curling strand.

"Ouch," she said, and tilted her head.

As she moved, her cheek lay for a second against his wrist, and then her slender fingers moved against his, each touch a scorching reminder that he had no right to the heat flooding him, no right to want Hannah Randall.

"There," she finally said. Her voice was husky as she moved back.

Sam's fingers slid through her hair. It was as warm and soft as it looked, the separate strands following his fingers. "Sorry," he muttered.

"My fault. I was clumsy." She cupped her elbows and glanced down at her sneakers and over to the tips of his crutches. "I'm used to Petey's sudden enthusiasms. Usually he doesn't catch me by surprise." Her face was worried as she raised it to him. "Are you sure—"

"That Petey won't be a handful? No. That I can keep him from landing both of us in the emergency room? I think so." Sam straightened as much as his aching muscles would allow. "But if you're not comfortable leaving him with me, I can understand. You won't hurt my feelings." He waited and hoped that she'd back out and save him.

But she didn't.

A done deal as he'd told her, and all the way back down the alleyway between their houses, Sam knew he'd taken an irrevocable step when he shouldn't even be walking, he thought wryly as he collapsed into his chair.

When he finally mustered enough energy to crawl between his sheets, he wasn't sure he'd ever move again. Too tired to stagger back into the bathroom for his medicine, he didn't expect to sleep. He expected his aching muscles would either keep him awake or in that twilight sleep as they did so often, especially when he didn't take his pain pill.

Instead, incredible after the way he'd pushed his body, he slept until the ringing phone jerked him out of his dreamless sleep.

Arnie, checking up on him.

Arnie, choking with laughter when Sam asked him to pick up a shovel and hoe and finally, grudgingly, told him why he needed them.

"I'll send everything over, buddy, but are you sure this is what the doctor ordered? I know I told you to develop some new interest, but hot damn!" Arnie's laugh sputtered out in concern. "Kind of a big change, isn't it? I mean, I still don't understand how you got roped into this, old son."

"Volunteered," grunted Sam as he worked his way into a clean pair of gym shorts and buttoned up his shirt. All his movements today were slow as slugs. He was paying now for the past couple of days. "You'll be able to get all that stuff to me before noon?"

"Hell, yes. Can I come watch?"

"No." Sam cradled the phone and began his morning stretches.

"Well, shoot."

"Yeah, and I feel like the target." With that, he hung up on Arnie's roaring laugh.

Sam spent more of the long morning on the phone. By the time he finished the last call, his throat hurt and his larynx was strained by all the talking, but everything was set.

Except him. He rubbed his clammy hands over his shirt. Why had he done this to himself? He'd had a choice.

Sam leaned back in his wheelchair. What was there about Hannah and her son that made him believe he hadn't had a choice? That they needed him?

He didn't want to think about anyone needing him.

Amuse Petey for a few hours. Only until Hannah landed a job, and then he'd go back to his solitary routine. No big deal.

No big deal, Sam reminded himself when the doorbell rang and he looked down at Petey's square face where excitement and anxiety fought for equal space. Hannah's fingers clenched in Petey's didn't do anything to reassure Sam, either.

She looked as though she were facing a firing squad.

"We're here," announced Petey, his eyes darting every which way. Waiting for an invitation to come in, he jiggled with eagerness.

"Here with a vengeance," Hannah murmured for Sam's ears only. "He's been wall bouncing since five-thirty this morning," she added as she reached down and traded envelopes with him. She screwed up her mouth. "I feel awkward, asking for references, but—"

"Don't worry about it," Sam said, pushing his chair back from the door. "Come on in, Petey, but wait here in the hall until your mom and I finish. Here." Sam handed Petey two card-sized, square, rattling packages. "Take a look at these until your mom tells me what I'm supposed to do, will you?"

"Yep." Petey collapsed to the floor.

Hannah rubbed her hands down her candy pink flowered skirt. She glowed in a reflection of Petey's excitement, and Sam wanted to tell her how pretty she looked with her pink cheeks and shiny enameled earrings, but he couldn't. Her shimmery pink top, full and loose over her small breasts, dipped into the high waistband of her skirt, and with every breath she took, every movement, the pink fabric gleamed.

The material would slide and shimmer like that, changing colors like a sunrise under his palms, her breasts delicate under the silky fabric. His callused fingers would be rough, catching against the sleekness.

"Sam?" The pink flowed up her long throat.

Bringing his scattered thoughts back where they needed to be, Sam cleared his throat. He flipped the envelope back and forth. "Emergency instructions?"

She raised her shoulders, embarrassed, and the pink gleamed, settling into the valley between her breasts. "Everything. I listed anything I could think of that you might need. I won't be long."

"Petey and I'll be here when you get back. Take your time." He folded the envelope. "The world won't screech to a halt while you're gone."

"What?" Her purse strap slid from her shoulder down her arm, and she grabbed for it just as Sam did.

His hand closed around her small one. Giving her cold fingers a little shake, he said, "Knock 'em dead with that smile, killer."

"Oh, sure, easy for you to say." She wriggled her nose. "They'll only have a hundred or more applicants for this job, some with their master's degree, and all I have to do is smile? Thanks, I'll be ever so comforted knowing that when they're running over my credentials." Creeping back up, the smile brightened her face even more. "I wish I'd known that before I took all those extra courses, though, Sam Dennehy. Where were you when I needed you all those years ago?" she teased.

"Growing up, getting old and tired. Making bad mistakes, that's where, Hannah."

Her face softened. "Everybody makes mistakes, Sam Dennehy."

He didn't want her sympathy. He wanted to tell her he'd made mistakes he couldn't right, had done things no one should have to live with, but he couldn't. Remembering in sunlight the night horrors he lived with, Sam said, "Hannah, Petey will be all right with me. I won't let anything happen to him."

"All right," she said, watching him with a baffled look in her dark eyes. "I know you won't," she added slowly. Her eyebrows curved together, and she looked frighteningly vulnerable.

A rush of terror made him add, "On my life, I promise you."

Her eyes went still, and Sam knew he'd been too intense. He meant the words, though. He'd needed to tell her he wouldn't let anything happen to Petey. For her. For himself.

"Go on, Hannah, you're going to be late." The envelope trembled between his fingers.

"Right." She nodded briskly, seeing something in his eyes that maybe he hadn't hidden as well as he thought. "Bye, sugar." She tilted Petey's chin up and kissed him. "Be good and mind Sam, or I'll snatch you bald-headed, hear?"

Petey giggled. "I'd look like Mr.—"

"Petey!"

"I would, too." He leaned against the chair's armrest and his small arm grazed Sam's.

When the door shut behind Hannah, Sam and Petey looked at each other. Petey's fists propped up his chin. "Mommy wouldn't snatch me bald-headed, you know. She just says that. I don't know why." He shook his head and rolled his eyes. "Mommies are like that, I guess."

"Yeah. I know she wouldn't, Petey. She was just teasing." Sam looked deep into the brown eyes so like Hannah's and knew all his worries about getting in over his head had only been the tip of the iceberg.

But it was too late.

Like a ship ramming into a huge ice floe, he was sinking. Petey's slightly anxious expression as he tried to reassure Sam that Hannah hadn't really meant anything by her comment shot through Sam like an arrow, ripping apart the last tottering walls of his defenses. The kid was too young to be appointing himself his mother's protector, and the shadows in his wide eyes shouldn't have been in a four-year-old's. Petey and Hannah were valiant soldiers in a war they shouldn't have been fighting.

Petey's behind waggled in the air as he balanced first one foot and then the other against a knee. "Now what? We gonna watch TV? I like TV okeydokey."

"Well," Sam began cautiously, "I wonder what you thought of those packages I gave you?"

"They make noise."

"Uh-huh. Seeds. Crooked-neck squash. Carrots." Wondering if they'd be forced to the TV after all, Sam waited. He didn't know diddly about kids. Ruthlessly he refused to let the memories come rising up out of the dark past. They could wait for night.

"What we gonna do with 'em?" Petey gathered up the envelopes.

"Plant them?"

"Yeah?"

Sam nodded.

"Okeydoke!" Petey's megagrin was an echo of Hannah's killer smile.

So plant they did.

In his wheelchair, Sam led Petey out to the backyard. "Past the tree, Petey, where the sun shines all day. Be too dark under the tree."

"Yeah." Petey nodded. "We need lots of sunshine."

Sam slid out of his chair onto the warm earth.

Arnie had taken care of the rototilling, so Sam and Petey poked holes in the sandy Florida earth, mounding the light-colored dirt around the seeds they poked in. The rows staggered drunkenly from one end to the other, but when Petey pulled the string Sam was holding tight at the other end of one row and wrapped it around a stick jammed into the ground, his look of achievement made Sam think there was a lot to be said for drunken rows of squash.

"You like carrots?" Sam ran his dirty hands down his shorts.

"Nope." Disgust ran from Petey's toes to the smears on his forehead.

"Well, that's what's in this next package. Let's plant them anyway. I like pulling them right out of the ground and eating them, myself." Pulling himself up, Sam stretched out the kinks in his back and reached for his crutches.

"With dirt on 'em?" Petey looked more interested.

"Damned right! Best part." Sam grinned. Sweat was beginning to pool at his waistband, but it was a healthy sweat coming from the hot sun, not the sweat that soaked him at night when he woke up from dreams.

"All right!" Petey high-fived Sam's hand resting on the back of the wheelchair.

As they poked the carrot seeds into the earth, Sam watched Petey's stubby fingers jamming them down, his mouth pursed in concentration. "You're a terrific worker, Petey."

"I am?" With one finger buried in dirt, Petey looked up. Then he looked back at the mound of earth. "Mommy says I'm a help. Daddy said I couldn't do nothing right."

Sam's throat closed. *Bastard* to say such a thing to this kid.

"He's prob'ly right. The kids at school say the same thing. I'm a doofus."

Sam cleared his throat and spoke more forcefully than he'd intended. "I know one thing. You're one hell of a carrot planter, Petey Randall."

Looking at the scoops of dirt for a long time while Sam waited, Petey nodded as though struck by some important truth, agreeing. "I am. I worked hard." He grinned up at Sam. "But you sweared."

"Yeah, I did. Sorry," Sam grunted, and passed the last of the seeds to Petey.

Petey stuck them carefully in the ground. "Mommy don't let me swear."

"Good for her," Sam grunted again, and wondered if he'd forfeited the rest of his baby-sitting hours.

He was surprised to discover he didn't want to be free of Petey. What he *wanted* was to plant his fist square in the middle of Randall Senior's mouth.

The surge of exhilaration startled Sam. Looking up at the blue-white sky, he took a deep breath.

"We done good, Sam." Petey rabbit-jumped to his side and stuck one sandy hand in his.

"Yeah, I reckon we did, kid." Sam closed his hand around the pudgy fingers. "We really did." He held tightly to the sandy fingers for a long time.

Late that afternoon, when Hannah came through the shadows of the alleyway calling out to Petey and Sam, she found them flat on their backs under the shade of the oak tree, a glass of lemonade balanced on each bare male belly, each brown head pillowed on a wadded-up shirt.

In the distance, a sprinkler rotated rainbow sparkles over a patch of earth marked off with string and sticks. The snick-snick of the sprinkler was the only sound in the lazy afternoon sunlight. Petey's left foot angled in to his right. Sam's crutches lay between them, and his wheelchair stood companionably in back of them.

Hannah stopped and her heart turned over.

The sight of her son stretched out in the cool wild clover beside the long strength of Sam Dennehy touched something in Hannah she'd carefully walled off.

She'd been right to let Petey stay with this man.

On her own account, though, she'd been careless. It would be so—so *easy*, as Sam had put it—to start depending on his solid strength, to start believing in *easy* solutions. She couldn't afford to let herself into that trap. She couldn't start counting on Sam.

Her joblessness was temporary.

Where she and Petey lived was probably temporary.

The situation with Sam was definitely temporary.

She could depend only on herself. Nobody else. Fact.

She must have made a sound, because Sam slowly sat up. His eyes held hers, and the astonished welcome in them stole her breath away. His smooth chest glistened in the dappled shade of the tree, and, as he stared at her in the humid heat, her heart skipped and banged until she could hear its thumping in her ears and then her breath came back, fluttery and fast.

A slow, drowsy smile moved his face. "I told you we'd survive." His voice was hushed, just for her, intimate in the shadows and sunlight.

"So I see," Hannah murmured. "You're an old pro at this, I see." She stepped closer.

"No." The light left Sam's face, and he turned to look down at Petey. "He's asleep. I don't know what kept the glass in his hands." Sam lifted it free and turned it upside down. "Empty." He ran his hands through his hair. "How'd the interview go? Did you knock 'em dead?"

"No."

"I'm real sorry, Hannah."

"Don't be. I'm not upset. I'll get the next job. Or the one after that." She moved toward him, her skirt moving softly against her legs. "I remembered what you said about the smile, and I came in second." She let the words tumble out. "It was terrific! In all the other interviews, I've been so scared and desperate that I think I didn't handle the questions as well as I should have, but not this time! This was the first interview I've been myself in, thanks to you, Sam Dennehy. You made me laugh, I wasn't worried about Petey—oh, I don't know. I felt as though I were sailing through all the questions. Anyway, I don't want to bore you into a state of blithering idiocy," she wound up.

"You weren't boring me, Hannah. I just wish you could have gotten the job."

Her heels were sinking into the soft ground. "Me too, but there'll be another job." She watched the shallow breathing of Petey. "How was my tiny tiger?"

"Quite a kid you have here, Hannah." Sam glanced at her. "His daddy did a real number on him, didn't he?"

"Yes," Hannah whispered. "But it's none of your business."

"Reckon not." Sam set his lemonade carefully on the ground. "I'll tell you something, though, I wouldn't like to run into him in a dark alley. Even hobbling on my crutches, I suspect I'd take after him. He didn't deserve Petey."

"No," Hannah whispered again, filled with grief for her son, but then she raised her head high. "He didn't."

"What kind of man is he, Hannah?" Sam swung over to her. "I've been picturing some kind of monster."

"No monster," she answered, thinking about Carl's tunnel vision. It had been there long before they'd married. She shouldn't have hoped that marriage would change him. She should have been smarter.

"You'd have to convince me." Sam's expression was hard. "He's not a man I'd like."

"No, I don't think you would," Hannah responded slowly as all of her past tilted in her mind, shedding a clear light on events. For the first time since the divorce, she admitted to herself that Carl really hadn't been ready for marriage and fatherhood. "He was just a man who had a different plan for his life than I had for mine. Finally, I guess, he decided that Petey and I didn't fit his blueprint."

"Did he do a number on you, too, Hannah?" Sam stopped in front of her. His chin jutted toward her, and there was an aggressiveness in his stance she hadn't seen before.

Hannah shaded her eyes. "No."

"Why do I think you're lying from the tips of your toes to your bright brown eyes?" Sam lifted a strand of her hair that had caught in the collar of her blouse. "Your nose'll grow if you lie, Hannah." He tapped the endangered nose.

Hannah felt that sympathetic touch right down to her curling, lying toes. "My problem if it does."

"Such a nice nose it is, though," he said regretfully, stroking the bridge of it.

His expression was so mock-mournful that Hannah couldn't help laughing. But her marriage wasn't any of Sam Dennehy's business, and she wasn't about to lay out the details of that pathetic little story just to satisfy his curiosity. She'd said enough about it already. She'd have to watch herself around Sam. He made it too *easy* to lean on him, to confide in him.

Taking refuge in distraction, she wiggled her nose at him. "Plastic surgery," she said, smirking.

His finger stopped at the tip of her nose. "I think it just grew a millimeter longer, Hannah," he chided.

"Surgery can do almost anything these days," she teased.

"I know." His hand dropped.

"I'm sorry. I'm sure you do." Hannah wanted to kick herself. Even on crutches, Sam had so much power and intensity that she tended to forget about his physical limitations. Another thing he made so darned *easy* to do.

"Don't apologize, Hannah. I'm grateful for what the surgeons were able to do for me. I would have been a heap of old bones if it hadn't been for them." He frowned suddenly. "That's true, you know. I *am* grateful."

She noticed his surprise. "But not always?"

"No." His eyebrows slashed across his thin face, and sadness and regret stared out at her. "I wanted them to let me rot. I wanted them to leave me in the wreck of myself."

"Why?" Looking at Sam's strained face, Hannah couldn't help asking such a direct question.

"So that every act of my life would be a reminder. That's why, Hannah."

Hannah heard the gritty pain underneath the simple words. Sam Dennehy had his own closet doors he wanted unopened, and she ached for the pain chewing him up inside, but there was nothing she could say. Clichéd words of comfort wouldn't help what Sam was keeping under wraps.

He turned away. His abrupt move caught his crutch in the grass, but he steadied himself and went over to his wadded-up shirt. Hitching it up with the tip of the crutch, he shrugged efficiently into the dirt-stained button-up shirt, his back to her.

When he turned around, he grimaced. "You ever wish you'd never been born, Hannah?"

She paused, wishing she could say something, anything that would erase the harshness from his face, but she couldn't and she knew he was asking her for an honest answer. "No," she finally admitted after thinking a long time. "There's Petey, you see. He makes everything worthwhile for me. He needs me."

"Lucky lady. To be needed." Sam's face was in the shadows, and the lighthearted teasing had fled.

"I know." Hannah wanted to go to him. "But without Petey, maybe I'd feel differently. I couldn't say."

"Well, we're getting way too serious here on this fine afternoon, Hannah Randall." He shrugged. "How about letting Petey stay here a while longer?" Sam motioned to the sleeping child, and Hannah wished she hadn't seen the loneliness in Sam's face at that moment. It weakened all her resolve to keep a safe distance from him.

"All right, but only until I bring over the chicken."

Glancing down again, Sam asked in a quiet voice, "Could you see your way clear to making it a picnic? For the three of us?"

Underneath the spoken words was another message, and, as if he'd said those words out loud, too, Hannah knew he wouldn't eat by himself. The food would be tasteless. Wasted. Charity, after all, she decided, to bring over food he wouldn't eat but would accept so that she could fulfill her part of the bargain. "You haven't had enough of my miniature interrogator?"

"I can stand him a little longer, and a picnic sounds like a fine idea." He shaded his eyes. "Petey and I want to stick the empty packets on the rows, and we have one or two other messy jobs to do. If we eat outside, I won't have to clean up yet.''

''Coleslaw and chicken it is. Picnic-style.'' Her voice caught a bit in her throat as she saw his relief when he dropped his hand.

She knew he didn't want to go back inside to his empty house. Well, who would it hurt if she and Petey spent a little more time with him?

All the way back to her kitchen, where a plump frying chicken lay on the drain board of the sink, Hannah told herself that she wouldn't let Sam become important to Petey.

Or to her.

She wouldn't.

As she went into her kitchen scolding herself, she let go of the screen door. Behind her, the slamming of the screen door had a hollow, mocking sound.

Chapter Seven

By the time Hannah had fried chicken and shredded cabbage, dark had fallen. Petey hadn't wandered home. Starved for masculine attention, he'd stayed with Sam.

With every downward push of the cabbage over the metal shredder, Hannah tried to sort out her conflicting thoughts. *Down,* little green cabbage strings falling into a heap. What if Sam became too important to Petey? *Down,* the pale-green-and-white heap mounding higher. Maybe it would be better for Petey's character if he faced whatever was happening at the preschool? She hadn't seen anything when she was there. *Down,* pale cabbage falling in slivers in front of her.

She kept coming back to those two points over and over until she felt as though her head would explode and she had shredded enough cabbage to feed a crowd at a political barbeque.

Finally, plopping a spoonful of mayonnaise and pickle juice into the slaw, she blew her hair away from her mouth and muttered, "Heck with it. So what? Petey's lonesome, Sam's at loose ends. He offered. No big deal." The sound of her own voice in the silence was startling, and she clapped her hand over her mouth and tasted pickle juice. Licking mayonnaise from her fingers, she decided she'd worried enough.

Sam would be a good male influence for Petey, who, heaven knew, needed a role model. There was no reason to expect that Petey would become too attached in the short time he and Sam would be together. So there. Stirring the slaw in time with her agitated thoughts, she whipped some of it out of the bowl and onto the floor, a clear message, she decided, that she'd done enough thinking.

Carrying the green plastic clothes hamper she'd filled with chicken, iced tea, coleslaw and hurry-up brownies, Hannah hastened next door and tried to ignore the way her mouth went suddenly dry at the sight of Sam's long legs stretched out on the dark grass.

She told herself that the longing rising up in her had nothing to do with the way his shoulders sloped wide and strong from his waist, nothing to do with the lingering half smile and questioning look he gave her, nothing at all to do with the way the air, even in the dark, quickened and brightened when she was near him.

And nothing at all to do with the way Petey sat leaning against Sam so contentedly.

"We're ready for a picnic," Sam said, and pointed. "Bring on the grub." He thumped his chest.

She walked toward the two. Sam's eyes never left hers. He just watched her with a look in his eyes that made her stumble once on the way.

He and Petey had spread an old blanket out on the grass, and a bucket of ice weighed down one edge. Petey's muddy shoes anchored the opposite end. Spotted in the grass around the blanket, they'd stuck glass containers of citronella candles and lighted them.

It was as though she'd plunged into an enchanted circle of light and darkness.

"Grub," said Petey, whacking his chest in imitation of Sam. "We want grub! We want grub!"

"Such manners. Okay, grub for grubby guys. Y'all look as though you did your planting with your faces." Hannah plunked the basket in the middle of the blanket and sat cross-legged on the other side, deciding for very good reasons that she'd rather keep a little distance between her and Sam, even a grubby, sweat-streaked Sam. Especially a sweaty, rumpled, earthy Sam, Hannah thought, looking where the rivulets of sweat darkened his shirt and the waist-band of his shorts.

Leaning over, she kissed Petey. "How was your day, sugar?"

"Neat." Petey grabbed a drumstick and waved it at Sam. "Best part. Mommy lets me have both, so I'll share with you, Sam, 'cause you shared your peanut butter sand-wich."

"A snack," Sam murmured to Hannah. "We were hun-gry workers."

"*Hard* workers," Petey said. "In a while we will have a harvest feast."

"A harvest feast?" Hannah asked faintly, as *temporary* flew away into the night.

"Sam said." Petey filled three plastic glasses with ice. "We will just have to wait and watch. And water. Lots of water. A garden is a big job." He nodded with satisfaction. "Big. But Sam and me got ev'rything under control."

Stunned, Hannah looked at Sam, who shrugged. "I've created a monster," he said, and ruffled Petey's hair. "Next thing you know, oh, maybe a cow?"

"Really?" Petey wiggled up.

"No!" Hannah and Sam said simultaneously.

"I was just kidding. Cows need a ranch. This is just a yard. Big enough for a garden, but not a cow." Sam grinned at Petey. "Sorry, bad joke. Garden'll be enough for a while, believe me. We'll have wildlife in it, rabbits, worms."

"Worms?" Petey was ecstatic. "Slimy, wet worms?"

"Afraid so." Sam's glance at her was definitely apolo-getic. And a shade overwhelmed.

"Been a long time since you were four, right?" Hannah handed him a plate with slaw and pickles. She smiled.

"About thirty years, some of them longer than others."

"Poor old man," she scoffed.

"Believe it," he said, and swallowed a forkful of slaw. "Hey. This is good." He glanced down with a look of surprise.

"Of course." She grinned at him. "But you're probably just reacting to the change in your diet. Dried-out chili makes anything taste good in comparison."

"Right. I should have thought about that." His smile grew wider. "Know what, Hannah?"

She shook her head. In the flickering light from the candles, his eyes were shining with something that looked suspiciously like mischief.

"You have three fireflies tangled in your hair."

"Oh, fiddle. I don't want to hurt them," she said, reaching up carefully.

Sam moved the basket to the side and knelt in front of her. "Hold still."

The light movement of his fingers through her hair sent sparkles up and down her. She shivered as his finger brushed the curve of her ear.

"That's one."

Sam was so close to her that Hannah couldn't look up. At that moment, she didn't have the nerve to look right into his changeable eyes.

She didn't know what she'd see.

Didn't know what he'd see in her eyes.

"Two," he said, and his voice had grown huskier than its usual scratchiness.

His fingers lingered at the edge of her neck in a long strand of hair. The back of his hand lay in the bend of her neck and shoulder. "Look what we have here."

Of course Hannah looked. His face was all angles and crags, and she could see herself in his eyes, knew he saw himself in hers. She saw the courage and endurance that had carved the lines in his face, saw the hunger and wondered if the hunger she saw on his face was reflected in hers. In that hushed recognition of loneliness and need, she couldn't speak.

The back of his hand moved with infinite gentleness against her cheek, and she wanted to take his fingers and spread them across her face, feel their roughness moving again through her hair.

It had been so long, so long and never like this, never with this sense of magic moving through her, floating light as dust motes flying through the air.

The blinking green-yellow light in his cupped hands broke the spell. "See, Hannah?"

The torpid on-off blinking of the small creature echoed the slowed-down thumping of her heart. Next to her, Petey peeked into Sam's hands, and there was a sense of such sudden completeness, such rightness, in the moment that she couldn't breathe.

This was how she'd always thought life would be.

And then she and Carl had married. Created a child. Divorced.

"I love lightning bugs, Sam," said her son, poking his head between them, and Hannah wrapped her arms around him and came back to reality.

Reality was a picnic supper shared for convenience in a neighbor's yard. There was no magic and no future for Petey and her here no matter how fast or slow Sam Dennehy made her heart beat, no matter how much hunger he stirred in her.

"They send messages with their flashes," Sam said, looking at Petey, but Hannah heard his words as though he were speaking only to her.

"What kind of messages?" Petey stuck a finger toward the insect. "What's he saying?"

"Oh, lots of things." Humor rippled through Sam's voice. "What do you think he's saying?"

Petey watched the flashes. "I think he's saying he wants his friends."

"What do you think, Hannah?" Low and running over her fluttery skin like soft sand, Sam's voice flowed around her.

Floating in candlelight in front of her, their faces watched her. Her son's innocent and curious. Sam's, lonely and filled with an adult hunger that reminded her of long-lost hopes.

Swallowing, Hannah said, "I think he's saying it's bedtime."

"Coward." Sam laughed in her ear, and turned to Petey. "We'll let him go with his friends, then."

Petey pulled Sam's fingers apart. "Bye, bug."

The twinkling light hung above them and then winked, blinked and was gone, mingling with the hundreds of other flashes spangling the night.

"Any interviews tomorrow?" Sam was back at his edge of the blanket.

Hannah shook her head. Maybe she'd imagined everything.

"No? Petey and I had made some plans."

Off in the distance, Petey made humming noises round the stringed garden.

"What?" Hannah focused on Sam's thin face. "Oh, interviews, well, yes, but I needed to talk with you about tomorrow because I have several. They're close together, and they'll take up most of the day. I can't leave Petey with you that long."

Before she could go on, Sam interrupted. "Of course you will. We are going to go fishing at the pier after we water and weed. Big plans afoot, Hannah. You wouldn't want to spoil them."

In spite of his smile, Hannah saw the tension that had him rubbing his chin and remembered the way he'd asked her and Petey to eat with him, the way he'd avoided going back inside his house. "No, I guess I wouldn't," she said, and curbed the pride that would have insisted on making other arrangements.

"Okeydoke," said Sam, and grinned at Petey, who'd crawled up on his lap. "Reckon we're going fishing, tiger."

"Reckon we are," said Petey, and stuck his thumb sleepily in his mouth.

"Cooking supper doesn't seem like a fair trade." Hannah stacked the dishes in the hamper while she watched Sam.

"No?" Sam shifted. "Hold on," he said to Petey. "I'm sitting on a vicious chicken bone." He held the wishbone out to Hannah.

As she reached for it, he held on and pulled her closer. "Believe me, Hannah, it's a fair trade."

The stark honesty in his eyes silenced her. She nodded. "All right."

"Make a wish." He gripped the slender side of the upside-down Y.

"No, let Petey. He believes in wishes coming true." Her fingers slid free.

"And you don't anymore, do you, Hannah?"

"No." Maybe it was the amber candlelight, maybe the lost look in Sam's eyes, but she went on. "I gave up believing in wishes a long time ago."

"Me too, Hannah. What about hope? Given up on that, too?" A sterile wind scoured his words.

Hannah wondered what had happened in that accident to leave him with such a desolate outlook on life, and whether or not she ever wanted to find out. "No. There's always hope. And hard work."

"Hope, huh?" Sam sat quietly twirling the wishbone. "Well, here's to hope and wishes, in spite of the odds." He stuck the wishbone between Petey's short fingers. "Make a wish, buddy. But don't tell."

"Of course I won't. I know better. They don't come true. But you have to make a wish, too, Sam."

"I don't think so."

"Sure. Won't work if you don't. *Promise,* Sam. I got a big wish to make."

Hannah watched Sam wrestle with his conscience and lose. "Pull away, kid. I *hope,*" he said, his eyes meeting Hannah's in a long look, "that all your wishes come true."

By hook, crook, or damned-fool luck, Sam wound up with the short side. Hannah suspected luck had little to do with Petey's winning. She rolled her eyes at Sam.

His grin verged, for him, on impudent.

Hannah decided she liked a rumpled, impudently grinning Sam very much. "How do you two plan on getting to the pier?"

"Oh, ye of little faith," Sam said, clipping the tail of her shirt with two fingers as she strolled past him to retrieve Petey's shoes. Holding her captive, he wound the edge of her shirt around his fingers and drew her closer. "Take a guess, Hannah."

"No car. Right?"

"Yeah."

"C'mon, Mommy, two more guesses," Petey crowed.

"A taxi?"

"No fun."

"Has to be a flying carpet, then, right?"

"Ding-dong, you're wrong," Sam said, pressing her bare tummy with one long finger. "We're adventurers. We provide our own transportation and supplies."

"Yeah." Petey nodded earnestly before turning to whisper, "How we goin', Sam?"

"In my chariot," Sam said, and waited for her reaction.

Hannah had a hundred questions, but she didn't ask one. She knew that if Sam said they could go to the pier and back in his wheelchair and fish, then they could. And Petey would be fine.

"All right."

Glancing sideways, Hannah saw relief wash over Sam's face, and the small sag of his wide shoulders. Folding up the blanket, she asked, "Want me to wash this? I still have your sheets at my house."

"Yard blanket. Don't bother."

Hannah lifted Petey out of Sam's arms. "Come on, sugar. home." Tucking him over her shoulder, she bent the basket under her arm. "We'll see you, then, ten o'clock? If you're sure?"

"Positive."

Leaving, Hannah didn't know what made her look back at Sam, but when she half turned, she saw him in the deepening darkness surrounded by flickering candles. He had lowered his head on his bent knees, and his interlaced fingers rested at the back of his neck.

One by one, the candles guttered out. Sam and the circle vanished as though the evening had never happened.

But it had. During the next several weeks, Hannah carried the memory of those moments with Sam inside that candlelit circle with her and let their magic sustain her.

The memory silenced the howls of loneliness and fear and gave her strength. She held the moments close to her like a talisman, and, as if in fact she held a good-luck charm, wonderful things began to happen.

Like a row of dominoes falling, one event nudged the next until she was tempted to trust in the possibility of happiness again.

And always, always, Sam was there to share the good news.

Three days after the impromptu picnic, she was offered a job. It was the one she had originally wanted because it was close to her house and it was where Petey would go to kindergarten in the fall.

One of the established teachers had become pregnant after years of hoping. "Forty years old and a first-time mom," she'd said, laughing, to Hannah when they met to discuss the year. "Lord, I'm terrified! And I'm ten years too late to use disposable diapers without feeling like an environmental criminal!"

But her eyes were soft and glowing, and Hannah smiled back, remembering the way she'd buried her face in Petey's belly and kissed him when he lay in her arms the first time, remembering the milky baby smell. "You'll do fine," she said.

The nursery school called and asked her to fill in for the last weeks of August. They had an emergency, and they would pay her for any afternoons she could work and over-time for any mornings.

Although the money would bridge the gap between her virtually nonexistent bank account and her first teaching paycheck, Hannah waited to give them an answer.

She wanted to talk it over with Sam first.

During those long, hot summer days and evenings, she talked a lot of things over with Sam.

She managed to overlook the niggling concern over the way Petey followed him around like a shadow. It was Sam this, Sam that, but Petey was sleeping like a log, not talk-ing about his imaginary dragon anymore, and Hannah didn't feel like rocking any boats. The happiness in Petey's eyes was enough for her.

She and Sam were sitting late one night on her porch. Pe-tey had already gone to bed, tired after another day of fish-ing and gardening and "stuff, Mommy, just *stuff*, you know" with Sam. At her insistence that their trade-off be kept even, Sam had finally and reluctantly agreed to let her clean his house in return for his keeping Petey on the after-noons she worked at the nursery school.

The only trouble was, Hannah told him sternly, that since he was never *in* his house anymore, it didn't need cleaning.

"I'll bring in a bucket or two of sand if it'll satisfy your pride, okay?" he said irritably. "Petey likes being outside, so that's where we stay."

Hannah translated Sam's grumpy assertion. *Sam* liked being outside. In fact, she observed that he spent as little time as possible inside the empty house where he lived.

"Don't make a fuss about it, Hannah. Please." He'd taken her chin in his hand, and his thumb had accidentally skimmed the edge of her mouth, a brief touch that had her lifting on her toes toward him before she knew what she was doing. His eyes had darkened, and he'd leaned down to her, his hand so still on her, and she'd sighed, and he'd backed away at the same time she had.

"Do-si-do," he said in his scratchy voice, shoving his hands in his pockets and leaving her leaning on the edge of the porch railing, breathing in the heavy fragrance of night-blooming flowers and swaying as though in the grip of a high hurricane wind while he disappeared once more into the darkness.

Afterward, through all those sultry nights of late summer, the smell of flowers came into her open window and kept her awake long after she should have been asleep, filled her dreams with sweetness.

Now, as she leaned back in the rocker, her feet propped on the porch railing, Hannah glanced over as Sam stretched out on the couch swing. His long, thick cane lay on the porch underneath the swing. Earlier he'd cautiously made his way to her house leaning on it.

"Where's your crutches, Sam?" Petey had been hanging over the railing watching Sam come to their back porch. Piles of crumpled paper surrounded him. He and Hannah had been making paper airplanes from a book she'd picked up at the library.

"Don't need them anymore, tiger."

A frown brought Petey's eyebrows together. Apparently, to his way of thinking, a cane didn't offer nearly the excitement a crutch did. "Oh," he said, clearly straining to be polite. He creased the sheet of paper in his hands and creased it again, shaping a lopsided wing.

"Watch." Sam sat down on the bottom step and swung the cane back and forth. The powerful swishing brought Petey closer, and then Sam, with one mighty swing, lopped off the head of a hapless sunflower.

"Oh, Lord," Hannah said, envisioning tall stalks of headless flowers.

"Oh, wow," breathed Petey, visions of who knew what running through his mind. The ponderous plane dangled forgotten between his fingers.

Sam unstrapped the brace and rubbed one knee.

As he fitted the brace with its kneecap hole back over his leg, Petey touched one of his scars. "Your oobie's better, huh?"

With great effort, Hannah managed not to interrupt her son. Sam and Petey had spent enough time together that they'd established their own relationship. She wouldn't damage it by charging in. Sam could handle himself.

"Yeah, it is, buddy. All that gardening and fishing, I reckon." Sam's answer was calm and patient. "I keep getting better and better." He didn't look at her, but Hannah knew the words were for her.

"Where'd you get this oobie, Sam?" Petey touched one of the longer white lines running across Sam's thigh. The white scar was more noticeable against the tan acquired from Sam's endless outdoor hours.

"Same place as all the others."

Hannah prayed Petey would drop his questioning.

Being Petey, of course he didn't.

"Poor Sam."

She stayed in the shadows of the porch, listening to her son's childish voice expressing the sympathy she'd known Sam wouldn't have accepted from her.

"Did you fall down like me?" Petey patted Sam's knee companionably.

"No, Petey, not exactly." Sam's sigh was heavy. Looking at the wobbly airplane in Petey's hand, Sam took it. "Like this." He lofted the white plane into the air.

It swooped and dipped before heading nose-first into the ground, the nose pleating back to the wings.

Stepping down, Petey retrieved the plane and looked at it. Sending it skyward, he said, "Sam went boom?"

The quiet crumple of the plane on the step was one of the loudest sounds Hannah had ever heard.

"Sam went boom." Sam reached out for the ruined plane. "Let's make one that won't go boom, okay?"

His voice was as tranquil as it always was when he talked with Petey. No one would have guessed from its even tenor that he'd been talking about a nightmare event in his life, Hannah thought.

"'Kay," Petey said slowly, and went to the porch for his book and stack of clean paper. "I'm sorry you goed boom, Sam."

For an hour Sam and Petey folded planes and flew them. Some didn't fly. Not once did Petey say *boom* when one of the planes crashed, nor did Sam say anything more than "let's try another one," but Hannah winced each time one of the winged white vehicles smashed into the ground.

Now, Petey supposedly tucked in bed, Hannah used one foot to keep the rocker slowly moving. Thinking about Sam's even reaction to Petey's questions, she finally ventured the one question that she'd thought she'd never ask. Sam's progress to the cane wiped away her caution. "Sam, do you ever talk about your accident?"

His swing stilled. "No."

"Not even when you were in the hospital?"

"No."

Unhelpful, his monosyllable should have stopped her. She couldn't explain why it didn't. "Why not, Sam?"

The question hung between them like the flower scents of the night. The sudden hiss of his swing moving on its chains was her only answer. Hannah waited.

"What do you want to know, Hannah?"

"Everything. Whatever you want to tell me." She dropped her feet to the floor and moved over to his swing. Her shadow fell across his face.

His laugh held no humor. "I don't *want* to tell you anything about it, but I will. I promised I'd answer any questions you asked. To tell you the truth, I've been wondering why you never asked me about it. I know you called the names I gave you as references, Arnie told me, but you never said anything. I let everything drift along and hoped you wouldn't bring it up." He sat up and grabbed his cane, struggling to his feet.

She knew better than to offer him a hand.

"Petey said it all, Hannah. 'Sam went *boom*.' In a very big way. But you knew that, didn't you?"

"Only that you'd been in a small plane crash and had a long recuperation. A lot of broken bones, months in the hospital after you'd been in a coma. A number of surgeries. You had your own crop-dusting business and owned your plane. Nothing more," she whispered through dry lips.

His cane thumped heavily against the floorboards of the porch as he paced in front of her.

Each thump vibrated through Hannah until she felt nausea rising.

"No one told you I was the pilot?" One last thump in front of her.

She shook her head and covered her mouth. More was coming. She knew it. The Sam Dennehy she knew wouldn't have crawled into a shell just because he'd smashed up his body and plane.

Whatever had smashed his soul had sent him into his solitary house and kept him there.

"Well, sweet Hannah, I managed to fly my little old reliable plane straight into the ground. Major-league *boom*."

Hannah watched him, watched the pain come back into his eyes, the shadows make themselves at home again.

"Well, you can see I survived." He gestured to his braces. "The doctors managed to pin me back together in spite of their worst predictions. Miracle workers. Wonderful men and women." The bitterness in his voice had been absent for so long that, hearing it again, Hannah flinched.

"Nobody told you about my passengers, Hannah?"

Once more she shook her head.

"I thought Arnie might have. To protect me, you. From the awkwardness, you know."

"Sam, nobody told me anything else," Hannah repeated while his words drummed into her hers.

"My passengers, brown eyes. My wife and son."

Hannah moaned.

"Nobody could put them back together. Everything ended in those last, desperate minutes for Rachel and Alex. I had to leave for a job right after he was born, and I'd just gotten back. He was only two months old." Bending over her, Sam gripped her arms so tightly she knew she'd see the marks of his fingers on her the next day. "I killed them, Hannah." He lifted his hands, looking at them as he flexed his long fingers back and forth. *"Boom."* His hands dropped helplessly.

Then, his eyes blazing and desolate, he looked at her. "I survived. And I shouldn't have. I should have been the one to die in that crash, Hannah, not my wife and son. That's the knowledge I take to bed with me every night."

Hannah tried to keep her tears inside. They wouldn't help Sam. This was a grief beyond simple comfort. Dark and cataclysmic, his suffering went, as she'd feared, soul deep.

Instead, she reached out and gripped his hand, took it to her wet cheeks, kissed his rough fingers that twitched under her touch. They had twitched in the same restless, futile way the night she'd watched over him.

"Don't, Hannah." He slipped his fingers free. "That doesn't help." From a land beyond her understanding, a country where pain shaped the landscape and peopled it with nightmares and regret, he stared back at her. "I wish it did, but it leaves me hurting more." He touched her hair so gently that the tears came to her eyes in spite of her efforts.

"Oh, Sam." Her throat hurt with the sobs she was keeping silent, and she was inarticulate in the face of his desolation.

His palm moved over her cheek. "I want you, Hannah. I look at you, watch you with Petey, watch the way your legs move, and I *crave* you, want you so much I think the nightmares will end if I can only kiss you, drown in the sweet river of your soft voice." Slowly his hand slid down her throat. "And then I lie down in that room upstairs where the only sound is the movement of the fan, and I dream of you."

Disturbed, she tried to halt his stream of memories. She touched his arm.

Unaware of her sudden movement, Sam continued, staring at her and not seeing her. "Sometimes I reach out." His hand rose toward her. "And I can almost, *almost* touch you. You're so close, and smiling, and I can hear your voice like music all around me, and for an instant, just for that one moment, I start to feel *happy*. I remember what happiness is. Then I touch you, Hannah." He was seeing her now, really seeing *her*, and his hands slid over her shoulders down to her wrists and up again. "And when I touch you, and I think everything will be all right, your face changes. You change."

"Please, Sam, I don't want to hear any more," Hannah murmured while tears slid down her face.

"You, Rachel, it's all mixed-up." He leaned close to her. "I see Rachel in that last moment just before the plane crashed and I knew I'd failed, knew she knew we were crashing, and I wake up shaking, wet with sweat, and know I have no right to dream of you, Hannah, no right to want you." The tips of his fingers trembled against her inner arm under the cap of her sleeve. "And yet I've wanted you since that first time I saw you out on your porch."

Hannah smoothed the hair back from his face. "I wish I knew what to say to you, Sam, but I don't. You've been through so much."

"And deserved every minute I've spent in that hell. That's what you don't understand. That's where I want to be." He lifted her up. "Rachel and Alex are dead because of me. For eighteen months, every ache and pain have been my punishment for living when they didn't. Every time I push my body until I can't move, I remind myself that *I* should have died, but I didn't. They did."

"Don't talk like this! It was an accident!" Hannah wrapped her arms around him to still his dreadful trembling. "You can't blame yourself for fate, Sam."

Stiffly his arms rose slowly and closed tightly around her as he clung to her, his cheek leaning against her hair. "You still don't get it, do you, Hannah? In that sweet, loving soul of yours, you can't imagine what goes on in my darkness. Sometimes when I'm with you, with you and Petey together, it's almost like the past never happened. Like I'm in a dream where the crash never happened, and I can stay in this dream space if I do *something*. Only I can never quite figure out what that something is."

He rubbed his cheek against her hair, and Hannah felt strands cling and pull on the stubble of his beard. She leaned her face into his chest. His heartbeat was as slow and somber as the tolling of a church bell.

"You're there, Hannah, in that daytime dream-time, smiling at me, and I get lost in your smile, the shine of your hair in sunlight. I touch Petey, and I forget he's not my son. Everything is new and fresh, and so real that I forget for a time what I've done. I'm happy. So happy that my heart turns over when I see you walking toward me, and I want to sweep you up and carry you off to that sweet-smelling wild clover under the oak and watch the sunlight move across your face, touch your body with gold while I touch you. That's what I want in those moments, Hannah, and my heart swells up with gladness, and I forget, I *forget!*"

His words took her to the oak tree with him, and Hannah knew how he would look, too, with sunlight in his eyes instead of the shadows that lingered in the greeny brown depths. She wanted to smell the clover crushed underneath them, *she* wanted to forget that the past waited for both of them. She wanted to linger in the magic of that leaf-canopied circle.

"And then night comes and I go inside." Sam's heartbeat was a steady, relentless drumming against her ear.

Held so tightly in Sam's arms that she couldn't breathe, his trembling moving through her, Hannah didn't know whether she was shaking or he was, and she didn't care. His pain became hers.

"I watch the ceiling fan circle and circle until my eyes blur, and your face swims in and out of my mind and I see the earth coming up fast toward me, and I hear Rachel scream. Just once."

"Shh, Sam." Hannah pressed her shaking fingers to his mouth, but his words poured forth, and she didn't think she could stand any more, didn't know how he was able to endure the telling.

"Not very loud, Hannah, just a small sound that I hear over and over again." His words scratched out the agony.

"You don't have to tell me all this," Hannah whispered, his anguish overwhelming her.

"For a long time in the hospital, I thought there was someone screaming in the room next to me. Finally I figured out it was Rachel. In my mind, you know? And so I listened and never let myself forget that she was screaming because of me, because I failed her and Alex." He turned with her in his arms and sank into the rocker.

Its old runners squeaked on the wood, and Hannah lay against Sam's wide chest listening to his heart beating steadily, carrying its grief.

Pain ground through her. Of course no one would be harmed if she let Sam Dennehy into her life. Silly even to consider such a thought. That was what she had decided so many weeks ago.

Sam's heart underneath her and the creaking of the rocker were the only sounds in the night.

She'd had no idea how much pain there would be. Hannah brought Sam's head to her and cradled him against her, weeping silently for all the nights and days he'd punished himself in his lonely cell of a bedroom.

Wept, too, for the harsh judgment he'd rendered on himself.

Chapter Eight

After Sam left, Hannah dragged herself to bed, where sleep eluded her. As though a cord vibrated between her window and Sam's, she felt Sam's presence. The moon traced its passage across her dim ceiling, and she knew Sam was lying sleepless watching the slow movement, too.

Once she went downstairs to call him. She let the phone slip nervelessly from her grasp. What else was there to say? What was she to do now?

Well, she'd known all along that she'd be smarter to remember Sam was only her neighbor. Nothing more.

More clearly than he did himself, she understood what he'd revealed in the quiet words that ripped apart that night. She heard the howl of pain boxed up so tidily in their hushed syllables.

Whatever he felt for her, for Petey, was too confused with his pain and self-condemnation for her to trust. For herself alone? If Petey weren't involved?

Watching the shadows, Hannah was terrified that she might step inside the dreamworld Sam talked about and stay there, keeping reality on the outside. Every time he looked at her, touched her, he brought her more alive than she'd ever been.

Headachey and tired, she got up and went into the kitchen for a glass of water. Like her house, Sam's was dark. Peaceful in the hours just before dawn. And, like Sam, hiding such sadness.

She sighed and poured the rest of her glass of water on the plant sitting on the windowsill and went back to bed.

For Petey's sake, she couldn't take any chances. She couldn't risk letting him become Sam's substitute son, no matter how her heart ached for Sam's loneliness, no matter how she yearned for his strength and wanted that humming sizzle when he was near her.

Petey was Petey. He deserved to be loved for himself.

She did, too, she thought a little forlornly as the shadowy moon faded from the ceiling.

The next morning, Hannah dragged herself out of bed and pulled on clothes. The sultry, heavy air bleached the sky to white, and everything she touched was sticky and tacky.

Hurricane building in the Caribbean, the radio announced, but she knew better. This was how reality felt.

She switched the station to one with a driving rock beat.

She'd been foolish and careless. She should regret the past weeks.

She didn't.

How could she? Sam had given something priceless to her, the knowledge that there was a man she could care for, lean on, trust.

She trusted Sam, his character, his values. He was a rock in a world of clay men. A man a woman could depend on enough to sacrifice a little of her independence and know he'd never let her down.

What she didn't trust was his emotions. Not enough to gamble on them and risk Petey.

Earlier in the week, they'd decided on a day at the beach to celebrate Sam's new driver's license. Sam was going to drive because he'd planned the adventure. He'd promised a surprise, something they'd never seen before.

She looked out at his driveway where the gray Jeep Wrangler had been sitting for four days now. He and Petey had taken the top off, put it back on, taken off the doors, put them back on, and finally decided on no doors with the bikini top. They'd washed it, waxed it and started all over again, Petey sloshing his rag in imitation of Sam.

Petey had declared that the Jeep was the neatest car he'd ever seen.

"Not a car," Sam had tough-guy drawled. "General Purpose Vehicle, buddy. That's how it got its name. *GPV.* The soldiers in World War II called it a Jeep because it was shorter to say."

"Jeep," Petey had said, and wiped down the side step. "Okeydoke."

Sam had found him a miniature replica. Petey had pushed it through the dirt, under the kitchen table and between Hannah's feet while she hopped from one foot to the other. She was Big Foot, Petey said, but Jeep would escape.

Jeep escaped. Hannah managed not to trip.

Watching the white sky, Hannah knew she couldn't cancel this day.

She'd tell Sam afterward that it was time Petey went back to the preschool with her.

Petey would have to handle it. She couldn't let the situation drift on. Better for him to suffer a small pain now before the case of hero worship became unmanageable than to be destroyed later after Sam sorted out his feelings.

She poured two glasses of orange juice.

Sam wouldn't brush off Petey.

He might. Once he'd completely recuperated.

Or he might turn politely indifferent. Like Carl. Only Carl hadn't been polite. Not to her, not to Petey. And that had been the proverbial last straw.

She took a deep breath.

She couldn't subject Petey to that possibility. He'd already turned into a three-foot clone of Sam, and Hannah had watched the transformation and ignored her twinges of concern.

Looking once more over at Sam's grassy yard where she could see the strings outlining the harvest-to-be, she had a sense that events were sliding out of her control. She should never have allowed Sam to make life *easy* for her.

But, oh, how *right* she had felt around him. In the gray light, she let herself remember those moments and knew just how much she would miss Sam.

If she'd met Sam Dennehy before Carl—

Then Petey wouldn't exist.

Hearing a muted thump behind her, Hannah turned around and watched her son's sleepy progress toward her in the kitchen and promised herself and him today. She would make today wonderful, and she wouldn't think about her decision until the day was over and she had to tell Sam. She wouldn't think about the tragedy he'd told her. She wouldn't think about the consequences of letting herself unfold in his presence.

Holding a once-blue blanket to his face, Petey trailed the rest behind him.

"Hey, sugar, want to rock and roll?"

"Boogie," he said, and stretched out his arms.

Scooping him and his blanket up, she whirled him around and around and around, dipping and swooping until they collapsed onto the floor, dizzy and laughing while the music pounded around them.

It was there that Sam found them. Drawn by their laughter coming to him through the open door, he'd come early, not able to stay inside any longer. Shading his face against the locked screen door, he looked in.

Sprawled on the floor with one knee bent and Petey half on top of her, beating his heels against the edge of the table, Hannah was flushed with exertion and laughing. Her Mickey Mouse nightshirt had hiked up under her, and Sam glimpsed the edge of white panties against the bright red. Her breasts were soft and delicate under the red cotton, her nipples tender bumps against the fabric. She was small and fragile against the green-and-yellow linoleum, and he suddenly, urgently, ached for her.

Sprawled in that splash of blinding sunshine, she was everything he wanted and could never have.

His debt to the past was unpayable.

In that brilliant, still moment of sultry heat and dazzling sunshine when everything came suddenly clear to him, Sam knew how important she'd become to him and how unattainable. She might as well be in a different universe, and he was caught between want and can't-have.

"Hey, Sam," Petey said, seeing him first and ceasing his drumming.

"Meep," Hannah squeaked. Tugging her shirt with one hand, brushing back her wild hair with the other, she scrambled to her feet.

"Meep? Does that mean 'good morning'?" Sam made himself smile, slow and natural. He wasn't going to let her remember the tragedy she'd listened to with such concern and tenderness the night before. Her tears had wet his face, and he'd tasted their salt on his mouth as he lay awake during the night. He wouldn't be the cause of her tears again. He'd been selfish.

"Umph," she mumbled, tugging again at the back of her shirt, trying futilely as far as he could see to stretch the fabric into respectability.

"Great. That clears it all up. Thanks." He slouched against the wood of the door and smoothed the wood of his cane. The polished wood felt as sleek as Hannah's long legs looked.

Meandering upward for miles from her slim ankles, over the smooth curves of calves and thighs, they finally vanished under the droopy hem of her red shirt. Sam could have stared at those smooth curves forever, that speck of white lace, but she kept inching back behind the table, scooting away.

"Want me to wait out here?" He tilted his head, feeling his gloom float away while he watched the flash and gleam of Hannah's first-class legs.

"Umph." Back into the hall.

He couldn't resist adding, "Nice legs, Hannah."

A flash of those remarkable legs again, and she was gone. He heard her mutter something to Petey, and Petey headed for the lock on the door.

"Hey, Hannah?" Sam drawled after her. "Why don't you just tie a belt around that and call it a mini?"

"Sam Dennehy, you're impossible," she managed to shout back, but he heard the laughter in her voice.

"I didn't eat b'fast yet." Petey's nose was mashed against the screen, and his mouth split into a yawn as he unlocked the door. "But you are welcome to come in, Mommy said. Want me to fix you some b'fast?" He yawned again.

"Thanks, but I ate." Sam sat down on a kitchen chair and hooked his cane over the back.

Petey climbed onto his lap and pushed his head until he found a comfortable spot against Sam's shoulder. "Yeah. Mommy says you are eating very good and growing stronger."

When Sam chuckled, Petey added, "She says that to me, too."

Tying a knot at her midriff in the yellow-striped shirt over her bathing suit, Hannah rushed into the kitchen. Legs gleamed beneath yellow cuffed shorts. She'd stuffed her hair up under a turquoise baseball cap, but the usual rebellious strands had already started the revolution and curled around her face.

"I liked the shirt better," Sam had to say, and waited for her reaction.

It came in a red to rival the shirt.

"Shorter," Sam said, and watched the red deepen. "And thinner," he couldn't help adding out of pure devilment.

She jammed the hat on tighter, glared at him and reached for a bowl in the cupboard. With uplifted arms, she was all curves, shining skin and rounded fanny. Sam liked the view quite well.

"Cereal, Petey?"

"Yeah," he said from the depths of Sam's arms.

"Petey, please. I've told you. Yeah is rude!" Hannah put the bowl on the table.

"I know."

"Why do you keep saying it, then, sugar?" Hands akimbo, mouth pursed in puzzlement, Hannah stared at him. The bill of her turquoise cap tipped over her quirked right eyebrow, and she shoved it back.

Sam started to clear his throat. Regrettably he knew the rude source.

Petey squinted up at him.

"Uh, Hannah?"

"Yes?" Her nose tilted just a shade, letting him know he was on her turf.

"Petey's like a little tape recorder, you know?" Sam rested his open palm on Petey's head. Such a miracle of bone and skin. So fragile, like Hannah, irreplaceable.

He tightened his grip.

"What's your point?" Her foot was tapping a staccato rhythm on the tile.

"Me. I say *yeah* all the time. I'm afraid I've taught the kid some bad habits."

Hannah's foot stopped. "Oh."

"Yeah," Sam said, and grinned at her. The day was going to be fine, just fine, in spite of what he'd told her the night before.

"I see." Thinking, she tapped her foot again.

Walking over, he'd been afraid she was going to tell him he couldn't see her or Petey anymore. He would have understood, and he wouldn't have blamed her, but the two of them had filled his life in ways he'd never imagined. Now he didn't know what he'd do without them. He would have to.

But not just yet.

Unable to restrain the surprising bubble of happiness percolating in him, he grinned again. "Bad influence, I reckon, right?"

Petey cocked his head. "Like how you learned me to make big burps? 'Cept you said not to do 'em in front of people." He slipped off Sam's lap and turned to face him fully, leaning on Sam's knees. "I remembered, Sam. I only make burps when no one's around." He whirled to Hannah. "Wanna hear, Mommy?"

"Petey!" Sam rasped, remembering the afternoon they'd turned belching into a fine art.

Hannah laughed. Her hat slipped off, Sam grabbed for it, Petey burped and Sam was right.

The day was fine.

Sam drove the back road into Bradenton where, just off the Manatee River, the South Florida Museum gleamed in the sun. He wanted to give them an outing, and he knew he wasn't up to a long, noisy day at one of the big tourist parks. He figured he could handle this comparatively small museum with its unhurried pace and friendly people, and he knew the fascinating collection of Florida things would capture Petey's attention. Leaving would be simple when either of them tired.

Sam remembered going himself as a kid to see the museum when it was underfunded and out on the pier. The first time he'd gone, he'd pushed aside the beaded curtain and faced the shrunken-head collection right at eye level.

He'd been hooked ever since.

They wandered through the clean, well-lit rooms, taking their unhurried time. They stared at the Indian diorama, Petey insisting that the fire was real.

They spent the longest time in the large, warm room with the four-foot-deep tank specially built and designed for Snooty, the manatee that had been a part of Bradenton for all of Sam's life.

The huge mammal held a mysterious fascination for him, this gentle, slow-moving creature older than he. Like him, it had survived in spite of all odds. Watching it roll ponderously in the water, Sam was moved once again by the creature's eyes, eyes that seemed wise and accepting.

"What's he eat, Sam? What's he weigh? How old is Snooty? Why is it so hot in here? What's he doing in his own pool? Neat!" Petey pulled at Sam's hand, tugging him closer to the chlorinated pool where the paddled-tailed manatee moved in slow-motion. "Can he hear us?"

The handler with the friendly southern drawl and the name tag reading Jane Hambledon strolled toward them. "Snooty can hear us very well. He has excellent hearing. No, don't try to touch him. He's very delicate."

"Big," said Petey.

"But delicate, too. He catches colds easily. He could even get pneumonia, if we didn't monitor the water and room temperature carefully."

"Yeah?"

"Sure. He's a mammal like you. He breathes air."

"Like me?" Petey sucked in air until his cheeks pooched out. Sam poked one cheek like a balloon.

Hannah rolled her eyes at Jane. "Children," she sighed.

"It's summer now, but if it gets real cold this winter, some of Snooty's outdoor relatives can die."

"Not Snooty."

"No. Snooty is well taken care of. That's why we feed him fifty pounds of food a day. Do you like apples?"

Next to Petey, Sam felt him nod.

"So does Snooty. In fact, that's how we get him to take his vitamins. We poke them into the apples."

"Mommy puts mine in juice."

"Snooty doesn't drink juice, but a lot of scientists say he needs fresh water to drink every day. He has a sweet tooth, too, even though he's all grown-up and not a little Baby Snoots anymore."

"Candy?"

"Bad for Snooty. Pineapples and strawberries, sweet fruit." She smiled. "We have some pictures on the wall if you want to look at them. Some give information about the difficulty the manatees are having surviving in Florida and the ways we're trying to help them."

As Hannah leaned over the pool and watched Snooty, her arm hugged companionably against Sam, and she grinned at him. "Snooty moves at your speed. No wonder you feel a kinship with him."

"Brat." Sam pinched her nose. "Snooty's older than I am, but we were both born in July. I guess that's one of the reasons why he's always been special to me. That and the fact that he's so rare." He turned to Jane. "Aren't there only a few left in Florida?"

"About twelve hundred is our best guess. There's the competition for waterways. Since they eat aquatic grasses and feed around the grass flats, they lose out when land is developed. Pollution's a big problem for them, too. Boat kills are one of the dangers we've had success in alerting the public to. Snooty has been a real help. Over the years, he's become a living symbol of the need to save and protect all of earth's creatures. Once they're gone, they don't come back."

They watched Jane feed Snooty and then looked at the pictures showing the plight of manatees threatened by fast-moving boats invading their habitats. Petey grew quieter and quieter. Several of the pictures showed manatees cut up by a boat propeller, and Petey stopped at the last one where the scars and cuts showed vividly.

"Boom," whispered Petey, and clutched Sam's hand.

Sam didn't know what to say, so he lifted Petey to his shoulders, feeling such a surge of caring that he thought his heart would burst.

Hannah stepped closer. Her hip bumped his thigh, and for a second her warm skin slipped against his. The warm humid room was silent except for the quiet slap of water on the side of the pool, and time seemed to stop. Petey laid his cheek against the top of Sam's head, and Hannah's hand somehow slipped inside his.

Sam wanted to hold on to both of them as tight as he could and never let them go, never let anything hurt this woman and child who'd somehow burrowed their way into his life and heart.

He wanted to protect them, but he was the one who could hurt them.

"Let's go, Sam," whimpered Petey. "But I want to say bye to Snooty first, okay?"

He let Sam lower him near the tank. "Bye, Snooty, I love you," he whispered to the manatee's bristly face, "don't get boomed, please."

"Hannah, I'm sorry. Maybe this wasn't such a good idea." Sam groaned, cursing himself for being a brainless jerk. He should have known better. Knowing how sensitive Petey was, he still hadn't realized how the pictures would link up in Petey's mind.

"It was a splendid idea, Sam, and don't you dare think otherwise," she said, holding his hand fiercely. "And I'm going to buy Petey a T-shirt with Snooty's picture on it."

In the gift shop, she slipped the shirt over Petey's head, and they left the museum, Petey touching the outline of the manatee over and over, whispering softly, "Boom."

In the Jeep, Sam turned to buckle Petey in the fold-down seat. "Hey, listen to me, buddy." He took Petey's hands in his. "Snooty's okay. He's safe in his pool. People work hard to keep him safe. *I'm safe,* too, Petey."

Petey stared back at him with those brown eyes that had lost their sense of invulnerability before Sam ever met him. They chipped right through the last ice-shrouded places in Sam's heart. Touching one of the scars on Sam's leg, Petey looked away. He wouldn't speak to either of them, just held the wadded center of his shirt tightly in one fist.

"What do I do, Hannah?" His heart cracking open, Sam faced her and traced the strand of soft hair by her ear. "What can I say to him?"

"I don't know," she answered, and twisted her fingers together. "Anything, please."

It was the strain in her eyes that gave him the answer and made him take the risk.

When they parked behind the chain fence of an empty restaurant's parking lot across from the local airport, Hannah's eyebrows zipped upward, but she didn't say anything.

Unbuckling Petey, Sam said, "Come on, buddy, I want you to see something before we go to the beach."

His free thumb was stuck in his mouth while the other gripped his shirt, so Sam tossed him up under an arm, held on to his cane and clambered awkwardly out of the Jeep, Hannah following slowly after them.

Stopping at the four-foot-high brick wall that had originally served as a planter, Sam sat Petey down. Then he helped Hannah up beside Petey. "You, too," he warned, and saw both pairs of eyes widen at each other, saw Hannah and Petey shrug together and make a face.

Standing between them, Sam let his muscles stretch out. He'd driven more than he'd originally planned, but the cramping was minimal. He rotated his shoulders. "There! Look now!"

A silver jet roared into the air and the pale sky. Wind and noise whirled around them.

"Again!" Sam pointed. This jet soared high, and sun glinted off its metal.

Keeping his hand stretching skyward to the endless silver stream of jets taking off, Sam finally said to Petey, "See? They don't *boom*, Petey. My plane did, but that was my fault."

He felt Hannah's arm jerk against him as if she were going to say something, but he didn't let her. She wouldn't offer sympathy, but she couldn't understand. He was the one who'd been responsible. *He*, not anyone else.

"I know some boats hurt the manatees, and that scares you, but people are working hard to protect them. They're making people aware of what's happening. You don't have to worry, Petey," he said finally, his voice catching as he looked deep into the childish brown eyes of a child who'd already worried more than he should have about too damned many things.

Finally Petey nodded. "You sure, Sam? Snooty won't go boom? *You* won't? Promise?"

"Petey, no more booms. I swear it." Sam tapped him on the arm. "Let me worry, okay? I'm bigger. That's my job."

When Petey nodded slowly, Sam looked at Hannah. Petey's attention was now completely on the jets rising and climbing into the air, and he'd turned loose of his Snooty shirt.

Hannah was smiling at Sam as though he'd just given her a present. Nobody had ever looked at him the way she was, as though he had the power to change the world. Her hair had tumbled out of her silly cap, and her eyes were soft and big with wonder, her flower-pink lips still parted with whatever she'd just said to him.

Sam couldn't help himself. He leaned over and kissed her. She tasted like flowers and honey and heaven. He inhaled the scent and taste of her, slanting his mouth over hers and breathing in her clean, sweet scent until her fragrance and taste filled him with sunshine and brightness.

Her mouth moving softly under his, she kissed him back, one slim hand sliding around his neck and curling there, her fingers under his collar, close to his neck.

Their touch stung him alive. Everything was springtime and in front of him, no shadows darkening the need he felt for her. He ran his hands urgently down her back, past the narrow indentation of her waist to the flare of her hips and up again, tangling in the softness of her hair. The dark sweep of her eyelashes fanned up and her expression was sleepy, and then she shut her eyes and tilted her head back. He touched his mouth to the smooth spot at the side of her neck.

Her short fingernails tightened in the front of his shirt, and she arched toward him as he gathered her closer, so hungry for her that nothing in the world was real for him except Hannah.

He forgot the sticky heat, the noise, the dust. He forgot he was parked beside one of the busiest highways in the state.

The raucous blare of a semi's horn brought him out of the haze he'd drifted into. His pulse still thundering hard and heavy in his brain and everywhere else his blood flowed, Sam looked at Hannah; she flushed, and they both looked at Petey.

Still watching the planes, he was imitating their unfailing
upward flight now with his hands and making engine noises.
He'd seen nothing. What, after all, had there been to see?

Two people in a brief kiss.

Not much on the surface. Not much to account for the
way his world tottered on the brink of something momen-
tous. It was the pounding in his blood that told the invisible story, though, and almost made him hope.

But of course the dust was still there, the heat, the past,
and so he said nothing. Couldn't, in honor.

Honor and endurance were all he had left to help him pay
the debt to the past, and pay he would. His life was the only
restitution he could make.

Touching Hannah's nose as lightly as the sunlight burning around them, he said, "We should head on to the beach,
unless you want to go home?"

"Sam, thank you for what you did for Petey." She held
on to his hand, not letting him withdraw it. "He's had so
many changes in his life that, oh, I don't know, sometimes
I think he overreacts. He's been better since he's been
spending this time with you, and I've been grateful."

"Don't be." He shook his head. "I don't want your
gratitude."

He hadn't meant it to be a loaded comment, but she
pulled back enough that he regretted not being smoother
with his words.

"What do you want? I've never been able to figure that
out." Her head was tilted, and wariness moved over her soft
face.

Sam ran his fingers through his hair and watched Petey
wing his palms into the air. "I don't know, Hannah. So help
me, God, I don't know. I can't tell you."

"What have you gotten out of playing kid-sitter? Have
we—" she hesitated "—been stand-ins?"

"What?" He frowned, confused and still caught by the
blood-thick hunger their kiss had begun. "I don't understand." And then he did. "For Rachel and Alex, you
mean?"

A small commuter plane lifted off in front of him. "See that plane, Hannah?"

She glanced at the field. "Yes?"

"As soon as I was able to sit up and move around enough to leave the hospital, I had Arnie bring me over here. He was my orthopedic surgeon. He became my friend. We parked on the frontage area. Nobody minded. They tried not to stare. Most of them knew me, knew about the crash. They left us alone."

Her arm had curled loosely around one of Petey's legs. Her knees were pulled up to her chest. "That must have been extraordinarily difficult."

He dragged up a half smile. "I made Arnie leave, but I sat there in that damned car for I don't know how long, forever, it seemed. It was hot, and I'd rolled up the windows. I stayed there until I could watch those small planes take off and land without screaming. That was how I mourned my wife and son." He shrugged. "You and Petey aren't substitutes."

"But you can't be sure?" Worry tinged her musical voice.

Looking at her clear oval face, so different from Rachel's sharp-angled one, listening to the low sweetness of Hannah's voice, Sam started to answer yes but he couldn't. He didn't know how to explain the bittersweet mix of what he felt around her.

"You're not sure," she concluded, and turned away, her hand securing Petey to her. She was silent for a long time, and then turned back to him with that killer smile that sent electricity running over his skin. "So let's go to the beach, Sam."

They did.

The gulf lay glassy flat. As though ironed, the light green stretched in front of them almost to the horizon where, far out, deep water began. Sam parked the Jeep, and they made their way to the palmetto-roofed tables out of the sun. Petey headed down to the hard-packed wet sand at the water's edge. Sam's cane was awkward in the fine, shifty sand, and he sat down on the bench seat, sticking his legs out.

He saw Hannah bite back her sympathy. He'd liked that about her from the first. She gave him room to be his own irritable, prickly, stubborn self. "Hannah?"

"Yes?" She was unbuttoning her blouse to go swimming.

A brilliant turquoise strap showed in the gap between neck and shoulder where her blouse had slipped down. Clutching the blouse to her, she glanced at him over her shoulder.

Unconscious, unplanned, a glance for shaded afternoons in bedrooms, and Sam responded to it. That half-shy glance aroused him so fast that his skin went tight and hot over his cheekbones.

He couldn't remember what he was going to say.

"Sam?"

He shifted. "Even in the beginning, when I was in the wheelchair, you never acted like I was an object of pity. How come?"

"If you'd seen the glare on your face when you opened your door, you wouldn't even ask." She laughed, but her eyes were gentle and warm. "Sam Dennehy, take a look at yourself in the mirror sometime. Nobody in her right mind would offer you sympathy."

"People have."

She came closer, and he could see the dusting of sand on her pink polished toenails. Sand powdered the narrow arches of her feet. He reached down to brush the sand off her feet, and found himself instead carrying one sandy foot to his thigh. Her toes curled into his palm, and her eyes widened a little.

A sea gull wheeled and screeched at the shore. In the still air, the slide of gulf on sand and Petey's voice carried clearly to them.

"Let me ask you something," she said in a constricted voice as he brushed sand off her knee.

"All right." He found his own voice going low and scratchier as he flicked tiny grains of sand off her calf. Her toes were a light weight on his thigh, but he felt their touch right in the center of his being.

"You touch me. A lot. Why?"

"Aw, Hannah," he said, and smoothed away the sand between her toes. "Ask me a hard question. Why does any man touch a woman?" He looked at her and smiled. In her blue hat and yellow shorts with the big white button, she was so small and earnest that he couldn't help smiling any more than he'd been able to keep himself from kissing her earlier.

She leaned forward. He could see the curve of the blue swimming suit top and a shadow of pale, smooth skin that disappeared into that brilliant blue. "Not any man, Sam. Not any woman. You. Me."

The question meant something to her that he wasn't following, but he knew it was important to her, so he struggled to find words.

"This has to do with your earlier question, doesn't it, Hannah? About being a stand-in?"

"Yes."

Her foot slipped to the inside of his thigh as she moved. He steadied her. "All I know is that I find myself touching you before I've even thought about it. I'm around you, you're there, and I want some kind of connection between us. I touch you and something happens. The emptiness leaves for a while."

"But that must be true for everyone. Every man. Woman." Her cheeks were flushed. A clear bead of perspiration hovered at the edge of her swimming suit top. Her skin was hot underneath his finger as he lifted the small drop.

"Was it true for you and Carl?"

She looked away, giving him the answer.

"Was it, Hannah?" He traced his finger down her throat to that same spot, where a second bead had formed.

"You know it wasn't."

"This hasn't happened before for me, either. I didn't want to be involved in your life, and I found myself letting you in

my door. I never intended to offer to baby-sit Petey, but the
words were out before I knew I'd even said them.''

He tugged on the still-tied midriff of her blouse, and she
dropped into his lap, her flushed face inches away from his.
''I tell myself to stay away from you, and I find myself in
your back porch swing. You tell me, Hannah. Why do I find
myself touching you every chance I get even after I promise
myself I won't?''

She murmured something that he didn't hear, so ab-
sorbed was he in tracing the space between her blouse and
suit.

He untied the knot in her blouse and slipped it free of her
bathing suit. He spread his hand wide and smoothed it from
the top of her suit to her chin, up her neck and back down
again.

''Tell me if you feel like a stand-in right now, because all
I know is that I'm holding you, Hannah Randall, in my
arms and if your son weren't within shouting distance and
if it wasn't a public place, I'd be trying to touch every square
inch of you.''

Her breath was minty and Hannah-sweet against his chin.

Off in the distance in front of him, Petey was a small figure circling back and forth under the dazzling sun.

Hannah didn't answer.

And Sam couldn't because he had no answers.

Chapter Nine

The wind whipped through the open Jeep and tangled Hannah's hair around her face. She'd given up on the cap because it kept flying off into the backseat into Petey's face. Behind them, the sun sizzled into the still, flat gulf, but the purple tinge on the horizon foretold the approaching storm.

Sun-blasted and sticky with saltwater and sand, they were all quiet. Petey, half-asleep, gripped a plastic bucket of sand that he said had a sand crab in it.

"I wish—" she began.

"You don't believe in them," Sam reminded her. His thumb rested against the inside of her wrist. "But if you did, what would you wish, Hannah?" His smile was lazy. His cheekbones were dusky red, and sand powdered his hair. She'd never seen him so bonelessly relaxed.

"I'd wish this day would never end," she said. She heard the wistfulness in her voice.

His thumb pressed against her pulse. "Me too, Hannah."

Just before they drove onto the bridge, she turned to glance back at the gulf and saw the last curve of the red sun slip away. Looking ahead again, she saw the road in front of them stretch into darkness.

Hannah closed her eyes, letting that last purple-red moment of sun glow against her eyelids.

The next time she opened her eyes she saw that Sam had stopped the Jeep in front of her house. The unfamiliar car in her driveway jolted her upright.

Sam kept his hand around her wrist. "Company?" The skin between his eyebrows had pleated in concern at her sudden start.

"No." She peered through the darkness. She didn't know the car, but she knew the license plate. "Not company." She swallowed the sour nausea in her mouth.

"Who is it?" Sam was turned protectively toward her. "Is there a problem here, Hannah?"

"I don't know." The edge of wildness in her voice disturbed her. She had to control herself. The storm had beaten her home.

He was sitting in her swing on the back porch, a handkerchief underneath his creased suit pants. His jacket lay folded on the back of the rocker. She could see the shine of his polished shoes even in the darkness.

"Nice you showed up finally, Hannah. My God, I've been waiting here for hours in this heat."

"Hello, Carl." She stayed at the bottom of the steps. "Why didn't you phone?"

He came down the stairs. "I did. If you had an answering machine, I'd have left a message." He stared at her. "Good God. What did you do to your hair?"

Wishing she'd had time to armor herself for this meeting, Hannah ignored him. "More to the point, what are you doing here?" Petey had crept up behind her, and the hairs on the back of her neck sensed Sam not far behind. An aggressive, ticked-off Sam, judging by the shadow joining hers.

"Daddy?" Petey stepped forward.

"Just a minute, okay, Pete? I want to talk to your mother."

Petey clung to the edge of her cuffed shorts, and she covered his hand with hers. "What about?" Sam's shadow merged into hers as he stepped forward. He'd moved so close to her side that the front of his leg grazed the back of hers.

His solid strength offered comfort and support.

"Why don't we talk about this in private?" Carl fanned himself with his hand. "Inside? Where it's cooler?"

"I have a fan. No air-conditioning. Outside's cool enough."

"You're being one real picky guy for someone who hasn't been invited." Sam's raspy voice brought Carl's head whipping around to him.

Carl gestured to Sam. "Look, fella, my wife and I—"

"Ex," Hannah said through tight lips, not moving and absurdly wanting Sam to stay at her side.

"Hannah?" Sam bent down to her.

"Look, fella, I don't know who you are, but this isn't any of your business, okay?" Carl rolled his shoulders as he strode toward Sam.

"Well, now, I reckon it is, *fella*." His cane bumping her leg, Sam limped forward. "Unless Hannah wants you here."

Hannah swallowed. Cane, limp and forced casualness, Sam had more menace in his little finger than Carl did with all of his rolling shoulders and jutting jaw.

"Look, this is between Hannah and me."

"Only if and when she says it is." Sam's voice was flat and nasty. He put one hand lightly on her shoulder.

Turning in surprise, Hannah stared at him. She'd never heard him talk like that. It was as if a stranger had materialized at her side, a cold, controlled, very angry stranger. Sam's face was tight, and the angles and planes prominent with hostility. Even though Carl was heavier and an inch taller, Sam, slouching next to him, still made him look insignificant.

"It's all right, Sam. Thanks." She let her voice tell him all the things she couldn't say. His being there had gotten her past the first bad minute, given her time to remember that she could handle the situation and changed her perception of Carl.

Carl had always seemed important and larger than life, but now, next to the shaggy, sandy reality of Sam, Carl drifted out of focus, plastic, unreal. She found it difficult to remember what had attracted her to him in the first place, why she'd given him enough power over her feelings to hurt her by rejecting her.

She had allowed him that power.

She had changed, though, since she'd walked out of the divorce court. For the first time, she knew how much she had altered inside. She was no longer a woman who could be hurt by this man's rejection.

His opinions didn't matter to her.

Except as the father of her son.

"I want to talk with Carl." She knew her smile wavered a little, but she was curiously lighthearted and free.

"Sure?" Sam's voice was rough and scratchy and for her alone, no matter who else heard.

"Yeah." She grinned, and he smiled back with a glimmer of understanding flashing over his face.

"I'm next door, neighbor, if you need me," he drawled, and she smiled back at him.

"I won't forget." She watched him limp down the alleyway. "Wait," she called after him.

He turned.

"Thanks."

"You already said that, and it wasn't needed the first time."

"Since you won't accept thanks, how about a North Carolina barbeque?" She watched his tall figure slouch a little. He must be hurting, and he still had gone toe-to-toe with Carl.

For her.

"I could be persuaded." He gave her a thumbs-up.

Hannah watched him until he turned out of sight. Then, stooping down to Petey, she said, "Sugar, you go on in and have some juice. Your daddy'll talk to you later."

"Right, Pete. I need to straighten one or two things out with your mom first." As Petey climbed up the steps and reached out to give Carl a hug, Carl held him off with an arm. "Whoa there, Pete, my man. You're covered with sand. I'm due at a meeting right after I leave here. You don't want me to have sand all over my suit, right?"

"Right," said Petey, and went inside the door Hannah had unlocked for him.

Hannah closed both doors. She didn't want Petey hearing them. "You haven't changed a bit, have you, Carl? Petey's great to have around when he's quiet, spit-polished and perfect."

"Still harping on that? Hannah, you're making a mountain out of a molehill. Damn it, I love Pete. He's my son, too." He started to jam his hands in his pockets and then reconsidered, letting them dangle by his side.

"You know, Carl, it comes as a surprise to me after all, but I think you do love him in your own self-centered way. I never thought I'd feel sorry for you, but I do." Hannah sighed and sank into the rocker. "You don't have a clue in the world as to what Petey's all about, and that's sad."

Carl shot his sleeve and checked his watch in the yellow porch light Hannah had flipped on.

She watched him in amazement.

"Look, can we drop this? It's the same old song, ninety-ninth verse, and I'm late because I've been waiting here for hours."

"Fine, Carl," Hannah said. "We'll do it your way. Cut to the bottom line."

"I had to fly in from Atlanta for a meeting in St. Petersburg. My parents drove up from Naples and they're staying at the same hotel I am. They want to see Pete. I do, too. I want him for the weekend."

"Nice, Carl," Hannah applauded. "Very concise." She turned on him. "Just like that? After six months of ignoring him? After not seeing him since the decree was final?"

He reached down and wiped dust off his shoes. "I let you have sole custody on the understanding you'd let me see him when it was convenient."

"Convenient for who?" Hannah said quietly, watching his face darken. But, when he didn't reply, she answered for him, "You, of course." She rocked quietly for a minute. "Do you have any idea what our divorce has done to Petey?"

"Drop it, Hannah. He's young. Kids adapt." Carl frowned. "He'll be fine."

"What if I say no? Are you going to threaten to take me back into court? Is that how you'll deal with the situation?"

Carl slipped his arms into his suit jacket. "If I have to."

"Not in a blue moon. You never wanted joint custody, and you don't now, so don't play these games with me. They won't work anymore. I'll let Petey go with you because I think it's good for him to know he has a father. That's the only reason, Carl, so don't ever threaten me again."

He was quiet, staring at her, and then finally straightened his sleeves. "Fine. I'll pick him up at eight tomorrow morning." He shot his sleeve again, and, not looking at her, said, "You've changed, Hannah."

Hannah didn't respond to his comment. "Petey'll be ready," was all she said.

At the bottom step, Carl turned to her. "You know I never wanted kids, Hannah. You did. Not me."

"I know, and I understood that, but Petey was more, much more, than just an accident to me," she whispered. "He was himself, special, *real.*"

"I'm doing the best I can," he said.

"Maybe you are," she said, thinking of Sam. "I suppose you are. That's what's so sad. Goodbye, Carl."

The squeak of the rockers went on for a long time after the purr of the car engine faded into the distance.

When Petey poked his head around the door, Hannah gathered him up into her lap. "Let's just sit out here for a while, sugar, and watch the stars while I tell you what your daddy has planned for you. It's too beautiful to go indoors. Maybe we'll just crawl into the sheets, sand and all."

In his yard, Sam heard Hannah. Sitting there listening in the humid night as he had so often, he was caught again by the music her voice wove around him. He wanted to hear her voice next to him all night long, low and slow and sweet like this.

He stayed on his patio long after she and Petey had gone in.

In the morning, Hannah's voice woke him. It was still low and sweet, but it held an edge of desperation underneath the control. Sam knew her well enough now to hear that little extra beat in her rhythm.

"He'll be here in fifteen minutes, Petey. Do you have your books and blanket?"

"I'm 'posed to go to Sam. We got stuff planned. I cannot go today. Tomorrow, maybe."

"Sugar, your daddy's here this weekend and he wants to have some time with you. He'll only be in town for these two days."

"Don't want to go with Daddy today." The high voice was stubborn. "Not going."

"Honey, you have to." Hannah's voice was patient and unbending in spite of the edge.

Petey's voice trailed off as the car drove up. "Sam will miss me. I am his helper."

Sam *would* miss him. Sitting in his bedroom hearing the voices carrying up to him from the driveway through his open window, Sam wanted to smash the wall down with his cane. Wanted to punch out Carl's handsome face with its razor-cut hair, too. Thumping his fist into his pillow instead, he let his thoughts churn.

How could Carl turn his back on Petey? On Hannah? He didn't deserve either one of them. The man should have been down on his knees begging them to let him back in their lives.

Then, hearing Hannah's polite, indifferent voice as she spoke to Carl, Sam smiled. He'd bet a thousand dollars Hannah wouldn't let him past her front door. Or any other door. He smiled again.

"Fella, you're plumb out of luck," Sam whispered and pulled on his clothes as he listened to Hannah's cool, sweet voice still rising up to him from the driveway. "Carl, old man, you played the wrong cards. You didn't know you held a winning hand." Sam didn't want to think about the meaning of the satisfaction swelling through him.

He smoothed his hair back and edged off the bed. "Tough luck, fella." His grin resembled a snarl when he glimpsed it in the mirror.

Without Petey, the day spun out in long, empty hours, but Sam went out to the garden, made himself weed, and waited for Hannah to come walking into his yard.

When night came and she still hadn't appeared, he paced around the yard, muttering to himself and from time to time lifting up his cane and whacking the grass. "All right, Hannah. Where the hell are you?" *Whack!* "Why aren't you over here where you belong?" *Whack!* "Come on, Hannah." The last *whack* split his cane against the oak tree, and he sank onto the grass beneath it, knowing he had a bigger problem than a broken cane.

He waited for lights to come on in her house, but it stayed dark. The house breathed, though, and he knew she was in there, alone. Sitting there watching her dark windows, Sam willed her to come to him.

Holding the splintered ends of the cane tightly in his fists, he focused on her with every atom of his being, knowing she would come walking through the moonlight to him, knowing she would sit down beside him and he'd smell the flower fragrance of her.

He waited, staring in front of him into the darkness until his eyes burned.

He finally went inside at midnight, leaving the pieces of his cane in the yard.

The next day, Sunday, repeated the pattern. She didn't appear. Her house was still and quiet without the bustle and music that characterized it when she and Petey were there.

But he knew she was in that silent house.

Finally, late in the afternoon, Sam glued his cane together and went after her.

"Enough's enough, Hannah," he growled when he saw her huddled in the rocking chair. "What in hell are you doing to yourself? You haven't left this damned house in two days, have you? And it looks like you slept in your clothes. Haven't eaten either, have you?"

He climbed the steps. "You've been crying, too, right?" he accused. "Why'd you want to go and do that? You look like hell," he said, lifting her up and settling her on his lap. "Ouch. Wait a minute. Damned cane." He moved it and settled her more comfortably in his lap and lifted her chin.

Her swollen eyes and tear-mottled face managed a smile. "That's a lot of questions, Sam." She blew her nose on a tissue.

"Nice to see you, too, Hannah. Now, where have you been?"

"Here."

"Great. Real smart. Sitting here feeling sorry for yourself, I'll bet," he chided, figuring on making her mad enough to spark a little sass. He smoothed the red blotches with his thumb.

"None of your business, and of course I changed my clothes." She blew her nose again and tried to climb off his lap.

"Nope. Neighbors share. You're staying right here. This rocker's big enough for both of us." He tucked her up against him and let her hair tickle his nose. "So why didn't you come see me?"

"Couldn't." Her voice was scratchy.

"Oh. Broke both your legs, huh?" He lifted up each leg. "Modern medicine's purely a wonder, isn't it? I can't even see the casts."

"Wouldn't."

"Much clearer. I really understand everything now, Hannah. Thanks a whole bunch, bright eyes."

She sniffed. "I didn't want to see you."

He reached down beside the rocker to the box of tissues. "Here, you might as well keep 'em close."

She clutched the box so tightly to her chest that the silver-foil box crumpled flat.

"Why didn't you want to see me, Hannah? I sure as hell wanted to see you."

"You heard us yesterday morning, didn't you?" She leaned back from him.

"Yeah."

"Petey didn't want to go with his father. Carl called me last night. Petey was crying and saying he wanted to be home with me. With you. I couldn't stand it. I'd been missing him so much, and he sounded so pitiful on the phone. He kept crying he wanted to come home and see you."

"I missed him, too, Hannah. These were two damned long, lonely days. Empty without you and Petey." He breathed in the sweet smell of her hair and tugged her closer. He snuggled her hip in to him and arranged her long legs over the edge of the rocker. "What's going on that you don't want to talk to me?"

"Sam," she said, toying with a button on his shirt, pushing it in and out of the buttonhole, "I'm going to be honest with you." The cool tip of her finger grazed his skin.

"Can't tell you how much I love conversations that begin this way." He blew away a strand of her hair from his eyes so that he could see her better. "Go on."

"I don't want you to see Petey anymore."

His heart stopped and he couldn't breathe. And then his heart began thudding heavily against his chest, but he didn't turn Hannah loose.

It had finally happened, and he wasn't prepared, not in any way, and he should have been. He took a deep breath. "Why not, Hannah?" he asked, but he knew, he knew.

"I think you're the best thing that's happened in my life, in Petey's."

"All right, you've soothed my damned fragile male ego. Now tell me why you don't want me to spend any more time with Petey."

"You're good for him, Sam. You know that." She doubled her fists in his shirt. "You're good for me, too." She pulled on his shirt for emphasis. "I don't know what I'd have done without you."

"Like vitamins, huh?" he managed to joke. "You'd have managed, Hannah. You were doing fine before I entered the scene." He was waltzing around the issue just like Hannah. He didn't want to hear her say the final words. The knowledge that something irreplaceable was slipping away from him made him hold her tighter against him, his fingers moving in her hair, stroking the cloudy softness that clung to his skin.

"You asked me if I felt like a stand-in, Sam, remember?"

"You didn't answer." He pressed her hair back from her face.

"I couldn't. I don't know the answer. I don't think you do, either, and that's the problem. Petey has a father, not a world-class one, but his father in fact."

"What does that have to do with me?" Sam took slow, steady breaths against the pain under his ribs.

"You're not going to be a permanent fixture in our lives. Carl, even though he's never around very much, will be permanent in Petey's life. Petey has to build some kind of relationship with his father. Lord knows he doesn't have much of one now. I have to give them a chance. For Petey's sake," she murmured. Her forehead rested against his chin.

"I'm no threat to Carl's relationship with his son."

"Of course you are. Petey's crazy about you. You're all he talks about. Carl is some distant, fading figure."

"That's Carl's problem." Sam felt as stubborn as Petey.

"No," she said, very gently, "it's Petey's problem, and mine."

"You said yourself I've been good for Petey." He rubbed his chin against her hand. "How can that be bad, Hannah?"

"You've improved so much in these weeks, and you're going to be going back to whatever is real-life for you, your business, your friends. In the meantime," she said, holding his shirt as tightly as he was holding her, "Petey is coming to depend more and more on you. It's as inevitable as the sun coming up that you're going to walk, with or without that cane, out of his life. When you do, and you will, I don't know what that will do to him. He can't cope with much more loss in his life. I'm not going to let it happen to him," she concluded in a strangled voice. "I can't."

The lump in Sam's throat was so big he couldn't talk. He wanted to tell her everything would work out, but he couldn't. There was too much truth in her words.

He held her and rocked in the chair and wondered what would stop the pain that was growing larger and larger inside him. After a long time, he made himself say, "I've hurt you. I knew I would, one way or another, but I tried not to. I let things happen. I knew better, but I took when I had no right to. I had nothing to offer. It was never a fair trade, was it?"

"For me it was," she said in a low voice. "I don't know about Petey. That's why we have to stay on our own side of the fence from now on."

"If I could offer you anything permanent, I would, but I'm nothing more than a hollowed-out shell, Hannah. Empty. I'm still trapped in the past."

"I know, Sam." She laid her forehead against his. "I know."

"It's the crash, Hannah. Guilt like a rock around me, pulling me down. I've mourned them, but I live every hour of every day with the sound of Rachel's scream in my head. Except when you and Petey are around. See what I mean about taking?" He touched his lips to her forehead like a blessing. "You and Petey gave me peace, and I took it gratefully."

"You gave, too, Sam." Hannah cupped his face, and her fingers were cool against him.

"I knew that peace was just an illusion. It couldn't last, and yet I let myself pretend that reality was the time I spent with you. With Petey."

"Me too, Sam," she murmured. "I wanted the summer to go on endlessly, just the way it was, but all along I knew it couldn't."

"I'm scared witless of hurting anyone else I care about." The words forced themselves out. "I won't let anyone else depend on me. I'm terrified I'll fail them, too." He shook her thin shoulders. "Do you understand what I'm trying to explain?"

She nodded, and he wanted to let her comfort wash over him, drown in it and never wake up, but he had to go on.

"I don't know what I'm going to do with my life when you and Petey leave. After the doctors put me back together, I made myself keep going. I thought I was paying for what I'd done to Rachel and Alex, but nothing I do is enough."

"Grieving is one thing, but what happened was an accident. You didn't cause it." She framed his face with her hands. "You don't have to punish yourself, Sam."

"No?" Her face was so sweet and caring that he wanted to believe her, but he knew better, so, doggedly he went on, trying to make clear for her what was confused and hazy in his own thinking. "I look at you and Petey, and I think of how life could be if things were different, but I can't get free of my memories."

"If it were just me," she whispered, her words low and filled with what he thought was regret. "But Petey changes everything for me."

"You know something, Hannah? I tell myself that life goes on and it's all right to feel good, but something deep down inside where I have no control doesn't believe those words, and instead tells me I threw away all rights to happiness in a few fatal seconds. That's why I don't have anything to offer you and Petey. One day, I'd let you down. I'd betray your trust.''

"You wouldn't betray me, Sam, I know that as surely as I know the sun's coming up tomorrow. What scares me is not being sure you know your own feelings, not lack of trust in you."

He had to finish while he still could. "You're right to end things now. I should have. I didn't because I couldn't. I wanted you too much to hobble away from you, and I still can't."

"You have to, Sam."

"I know." He slid his palms under her shirt against her warm, silky skin. She was so alive, and she had raised him from the dead. "Carl's a fool."

"I know," she echoed him. "It just took me a while to figure it out. But even so, I have to give him the chance to do whatever fathering he's capable of. Petey needs that from Carl. Petey needs to know that Carl has some feelings for him, and that won't happen unless I make it as *easy*—'' she laughed tearfully ''—for Carl as possible. I think he might do okay on a short-term basis. It's just the day-to-day slugging it out in the trenches he can't handle." She rubbed her face against him, and Sam didn't think he could stand the pain.

"Oh God, Hannah. I wish things were different." He sent that wish winging out into the universe, knowing it would never be answered. In a few minutes, he was going to have to stand up and limp out of her life.

He would do it because walking away from her and Petey was all that Hannah needed from him.

He would do what she asked because it was all he could give her.

Chapter Ten

After Sam left, Hannah's house was tomblike quiet, but once Petey was home, she'd be fine.

Passing through the kitchen, Hannah turned the radio on loud. She wanted noise, lots of it. Whatever midsummer's dream she'd been living in was over. Over, she muttered to herself. *Fini.* The words were astringent splashed on a razor cut.

She'd done the right thing.

She'd done the only thing she could do for Petey.

She'd made herself stay away from Sam until he'd come to her back porch. She could do it again.

Grabbing a quart of vinyl paper paste, she headed up to the almost-finished bathroom that had been waiting for her for weeks.

Two days of moping around an empty house were enough for any self-respecting woman, she told herself. Moping didn't solve anything.

The border was going up.

When Petey returned Sunday night, the border was up, and every radio in the house was blasting out music, news and weather. If she'd had a TV, it would have been on, too.

Carl didn't say when he'd see Petey again.

With his thumb in his mouth, Petey watched from the window until Carl's car left.

"Did you have a nice time, sugar?" Hannah asked when he let the shade fall.

"Daddy was very busy," he answered. "Not like Sam."

"What about Nana and Papa?" Hannah liked them although she'd never gotten to know them during her marriage.

"Nana and Papa don't like to play games or tell stories. I'm going to Sam's now," he announced, and headed to the back door.

"Not tonight, sugar. It's too late." Hannah couldn't tell him about Sam. Not yet. Not while he was a sleepy, sad lump in her arms.

"Not for Sam. I missed him and I knowed he missed me."

"Yes, he did, but we'll talk about Sam tomorrow." Hannah's stomach twinged.

Hannah fed Petey until his stomach was round and hard, told him stories until her throat was sore, and sat by his bed until he fell asleep. She was happy and relieved to have him home.

So happy and relieved, in fact, that she scolded herself for feeling as though something were still missing.

The Caribbean storm stalled, and so did Monday morning when Hannah sat Petey down and told him that it was time he went back to nursery school.

"No. Sam's is where I go now." He looked anxious.

Hannah groaned. She wished Petey hadn't inherited her stubbornness. She began again.

In the driveway before he climbed into the car, Petey stared a long time at Sam's house, its shade-covered windows. "Sam don't like me no more?" His small shoulders drooped.

"Sugar, Sam likes you. You know he does. But Sam's almost well now, and he has to get back to work. He has things to do."

"Like Daddy." Petey clicked the seat belt around him.

Hannah looked up at Sam's bedroom window. It was cracked open. She prayed Sam hadn't heard Petey's woeful comment.

She'd been right to end their reliance on Sam, she told herself. Petey's reaction proved that. Sam's eventual departure would have devastated Petey.

Sam didn't let himself watch from his window. That would have been cheating. He couldn't help hearing, though, and the stabbing pain fought with all the old body pains and the suffocating guilt for room in his overburdened heart.

He couldn't stay here and keep away from them. Hannah didn't deserve that. Nor did Petey. Day after day, trying to avoid Hannah and her son, Sam made a decision.

He would find another place to live.

He had to.

The storm played hide-and-seek, threatening, stalling, building. The weather stayed oppressive and gummy. Some days Hannah couldn't breathe. In the supersaturated air, taking a breath was like breathing underwater.

She got up each day with leaden feet and heart, moving through the heavy stickiness of the late-summer days with forced energy and false enthusiasm.

Like an apprentice burglar, she began casing Sam's house, watching for any glimpse of him, but telling herself that seeing him would be like putting a drink in front of an alcoholic. Too cruel.

Once, she caught a glimpse of Sam's nightly cigar arcing through the darkness and smelled its smoke. When she caught herself inhaling the smell of smoke hungrily, she didn't go out on her porch anymore after she put Petey to bed.

Petey was too quiet. When he did talk, he only wanted to talk about the things he and Sam had done during the summer. Hannah listened to the stories and ached for all that Sam had given to Petey.

On a day clammy with heat and humidity, she saw Sam, his gaze on the ground, limp out to a car waiting in his driveway. Hannah waited, wanting him to look her way, dreading that he would.

He didn't, and the car disappeared into the shimmering heat. That night and the next, Sam's house was a looming, empty presence next to hers, and her loneliness was a living, breathing creature growing inside her.

As the storm finally made up its mind to be a hurricane and headed for the Texas coast, sideswiping the west coast of Florida with wind and rain, Hannah realized that Sam had truly gone.

His house stayed dark, and there were no mail deliveries for him. She knew because she watched.

That was the night Petey woke up and found her weeping into her turquoise baseball cap.

"You miss Sam, too?" He crawled into her lap.

Through the driving rain, Hannah looked out at Sam's empty house. It looked as if Sam had never lived there. "Yes, sugar."

"Jeep's gone."

"I know. Sam, too."

"Sam and me never cooked our harvest. I peek through the fence and watch our garden. Nobody's weeded it. It needed water, but this storm is gonna drown all the squashes."

"Oh, Petey." Hannah swallowed her tears. She'd thought Petey would get over Sam. She'd thought she would, too, but the aching emptiness inside her was growing larger each day, gnawing away at her. "We'll cook a harvest, okay?"

"No. Won't be the same. You and me didn't growed a harvest."

"No," Hannah whispered, "it wouldn't be the same."

"Everything is bad without Sam. And badder." Petey butted his head under her chin. "I miss Sam, and I wish he didn't leave. I'm scared he goed *boom* again, Mommy, and I want him back." Petey wound his arms around her neck.

"Me too, sugar." She'd waited too long to send Sam away, and now the damage was done. She'd made the biggest mistake of her life. "But there's nothing we can do." She wiped her eyes with the bill of her cap.

"Nothing we can do," Petey agreed, but his face had a distant expression, and Hannah was afraid he was going to start talking about his dragon again. He only looked at her, though, with that same faraway look in his eyes and went back up to bed.

For two days, the rain continued, steadily drumming down while Calliope battered the Texas coast, retreating and returning again to savage the low-lying areas.

Hannah's street was flooded, and her yard ankle deep in water by the time the storm whirled into oblivion. She dragged out the mildewed clothes from the closets and laid them out in the sunshine to dry. Sam's yard had fared better than hers, she noticed, and the garden was lifting rain-pummmeled leaves to the sun.

"Will Sam come home?" Petey pulled at her arm.

"I don't know, honey. I don't think so." And Hannah, who'd given up on wishing, made her first real wish since childhood. "I wish he would, Petey, more than anything, I *wish* Sam would come ambling down our alleyway."

She didn't expect him to.

He didn't.

What would she have told him anyway? That she could wait while he sorted out his emotions? And what if he never did?

She fixed supper and almost set three places. "Great, Hannah. Why don't you just put a front-page ad in the paper and tell Sam you want to see him?" Slamming the cupboard door on the offending plate now resting on the shelf, she scowled at the table set for two.

She'd let Petey go out in the yard after most of the water had drained away, and he stayed there all afternoon, peeking through the fence, standing on an old tree stump she should dig up and whacking randomly with a stick at the sunflowers lifting their heavy heads to the sky.

After they ate, he went back out into the dark. Hannah cleaned the kitchen and muttered to herself. "Damn you, Sam Dennehy. If I ever get my hands on you again, I swear, I swear— I don't know what I'd do with you. Something. I'd make you listen to me, that's for sure." She flipped the radio on.

The song was a slow and sexy ballad about lovers in the night. She spun through the stations until she found a pile-driving rap number whose lyrics she couldn't understand.

Outside, the mosquitoes buzzed around Petey's neck, but he didn't care. He'd wait until the dragon came if he had to stay out all night.

He must have fallen asleep because he never heard the dragon, just smelled his smoke. Petey looked through the fence and saw the lingering movement of the dragon's red eye.

"Hey, it's me," he whispered.

"Petey," came the dragon's familiar rasp. It held sadness and a world of loneliness.

Petey knew how the dragon felt. "Yeah, me."

The dragon's sigh was heavy, and his eye flared. "Yeah."

Petey wiggled to get a better look. "You left."

"I did." The dragon moved with a muffled thump. "Go on home, Petey. I want to be alone."

"You got to help me first," Petey said, anxiety running through him. "I need you."

There was a long, buzz-filled silence before the dragon answered. "I can't help, Petey. I'm going to be leaving soon."

"But you can, you got to," Petey wailed, his voice rising. "Mommy and me miss Sam. Make Sam come back to us!"

"It's impossible. You don't understand." The glowing eye was close to the ground. "I can't do that."

"You fixed stuff before. Mommy and me *need* Sam. We want Sam to come home. He belongs here, and we can't get along without him. We miss him and we're sad without him."

"Sam's sad, too." His voice was low. "But I can't change things, Petey." The gravelly voice was harsh. There was a grating sound, and the dragon said, "Go home where you belong, Petey. Forget about me." His hot eye lifted and sank to the ground.

"No!" Petey screamed, and pulled at the fence. Kicking the fence and digging his feet and hands into the knotty spaces, he pulled himself to the top. "Wait!"

Inside, Hannah heard Petey's scream and turned, her mind blank and frozen with fear. Then she dropped the dish she was drying and ran.

At his patio door, Sam heard Petey's scream and turned. The small dark shape scrambling to the top of his fence sent his heart roaring into his ears. "Hell! Petey! Don't move," Sam yelled, and ran for him.

It was like the crash all over. His body wouldn't obey his commands. Pounding his cane into the ground as fast as he could, Sam saw Petey totter on the edge. "Petey! Hold on!" he shouted, and flung the cane to the side as he stretched his arms out to the child.

"Sam!" Petey's joyful cry rang through the night. He jerked upright, turning away from the backyard toward the house.

He tumbled to the ground from the eight-foot fence, but to Sam, watching and hurrying to catch him, Petey moved in slow-motion darkness to the ground.

"Damn it to hell, Petey!" Sam grabbed for him and tagged the heel of his foot.

Petey's body hit the ground with an enormous whump and lay still.

Stumbling across the yard, Hannah heard Sam swear at Petey and whirled frantically, looking for them.

Sam's steady stream of self-directed curses sent her racing down the alleyway separating their houses and pelting into his yard. Back by the fence, Sam was bent over a small lump on the wet ground.

"Petey!" Hannah shrieked, and ran blindly through the dark to him and Sam.

"Hannah, listen to me," Sam's voice came to her as she ran. He was icy calm and distant. "He's breathing. I don't see any blood. Go inside and call the hospital emergency room. Tell them we're on our way. He's unconscious. They'll need X rays. Ask them to call Arnie Reynolds and have him meet us there. Bring me that board by the back door. I'll slide it under him and have him in the Jeep by the time you've called."

Hannah touched Petey's closed eyes with shaking, icy fingers. "All right," she whimpered. When she returned with the board, Sam moved quickly to ease Petey on the board without jostling him and steadied his head with the dish towel Hannah still clutched in her shaking fingers.

"The phone number of the hospital emergency room is by the phone, Hannah. Meet me in front. If I get Petey in the Jeep before you come out, I'll go on and you meet me there, hear? It will be faster," he said as he staggered upright with Petey lying still and unmoving on the board.

Hannah managed to climb into the Jeep just before Sam pulled out. She crouched in the back with Petey and, terrified to move him, gripped the tips of his fingers.

In the fluorescent lights around the emergency room, she saw Sam's sickly white face and tight mouth. The rest of the night was a blur of gurneys and blue gowns moving past her. She stayed with Petey, never turning loose of his fingers until Reynolds, the orthopedic surgeon Sam had asked for, Sam's friend, shooed her into the hall. Sam followed, his face still that washed-out white.

"No concussion. A cracked collarbone. No internal bleeding, thank God."

Hannah sagged, and Sam's arm under her elbow kept her from crumpling to the floor. "He's going to be okay?" she murmured while the green-tiled room circled in front of her. Sam's arm around her waist was the only solid thing in the whirling colors in front of her eyes. He had stayed close to her from the moment they'd rushed through the wide sliding doors of the emergency room. Now, his hand on her back, he pushed her into a chair while the doctor waited with a huge grin on his round face. "He's going to be okay?" she repeated, needing to hear the words again.

"Sure. This guy's indestructible. Also, the wet ground apparently helped cushion his fall. I want to check him over again after we fix him up with a collar harness, but then we'll let you take the Flying Bambino home. You've got a real fun six weeks ahead with this little squirt. Limited movement, and from what Sam tells me, the kid's not much for sitting still." Reynolds's stocky figure squatted in front of her. "Hey, not to worry. He's fine."

Hannah lifted her head in spite of Sam's hand pressing it down between her knees.

Reynolds's light blue eyes were understanding. "Really, he's out of the woods. I only want to see how he is with the harness, double-check, you know." He patted her awkwardly on the back and stood up. His knees creaked. "Woof. Got to get back to running. Sam, can I see you for a second?"

Resting her head on her arms, Hannah heard the off-beat rhythm of Sam's stride, the muffled crump of the doctor's soft-soled shoes. With a great outrush, energy drained from her. Like a rag doll, she slumped in the plastic seat.

When Sam returned, his slow steps stopped in front of her. His sneakered feet were inches away from her bare toes.

She'd been barefoot the whole time and not known it.

"Hannah, Arnie said you can go back in and wait with Petey for the nurse to set him up with the harness."

Reaching out, she took his hand. Firm and solid, it anchored her. "What would I have done without you?"

His finger twitched. "I should have caught him. I didn't. I screwed up."

Dazed, Hannah looked at him, really looked at him for the first time since she'd seen him kneeling over Petey. Sam's eyes were tormented. "What are you talking about?" She pressed her palms to her eyes. "You're not making sense."

"My fault he's hurt. I should have done something."

"What?" Hannah shook her head. Sam might as well be speaking a foreign language, for all the sense his words were making to her.

"Look, Hannah, I let him get hurt. I told you a long time ago to take your precious son and run like hell away from me. You should have. Petey's lying in there because of me." His hands twitched in front of her, and his eyes were sunken.

Anger pushed out Hannah's exhaustion and shot her to her feet. "You're crazy, Sam. You were the one who organized everything so that I didn't have to worry. *You* made it possible for Petey to be treated so quickly."

"I didn't catch him." Sam's voice was harsh and abrasive. "He was climbing my fence, and I didn't catch him."

"Kids climb fences, Sam. All the time. Trees, fences, tables! That's what kids do." She grabbed his restless fingers and stilled them with hers.

"I failed him."

She almost missed the words. "Is that what this is all about, Sam? The crash? Petey's fall? One more chance to beat yourself up? Punish yourself for some imagined failure?"

He tried to turn away, but she saw his bleak expression and wouldn't let him. "Let me go, Hannah. You don't know what you're talking about."

She grabbed his shirt and pulled until he faced her. "Why aren't you blaming *me* if you want to blame someone? Kids have to be watched like a hawk all the time. I was in the kitchen. Why wasn't his accident *my* fault, Sam? How dare you give me a pass and shoulder blame when there isn't any? Answer me!" She shook his shirt a little, but he wouldn't respond. "I know what you're trying to do, and you're wrong, Sam Dennehy, wrong!"

"What do you think I'm doing, Hannah?" He glared at her, his anger crashing against hers.

"I think you're taking everything on your own shoulders. Just the way you did for the plane crash."

"I don't want to talk about this right now." His anger chased the desolation from his hazel eyes.

"I do." She wasn't going to let him off the hook.

"I've said everything I can." Desperation gleamed at her, Sam hiding behind a wall.

"I haven't. You still haven't answered me. Why aren't you blaming *me* for Petey's accident? Tell me, Sam!" She gave his shirt a little shake.

"You weren't to blame." He was so stubborn he reminded her of Petey.

"No? I'm his mother. I said he could go outside. *My* fault he was hurt, isn't it?"

"No."

"Not yours, either, Sam," she said, and let her voice soften in the face of his agony. "Petey's in there because he climbed a fence and fell. He's hurt because of an *accident*. Not because I was a bad mother. Not because you *failed*. You've been there for Petey, for me, every time I turned around. You brought something into my life I'd given up on. You never failed. Petey's fall was no more your fault than the plane crash."

He stared at her from behind a wall of old grief and punishment.

"Tell me, Sam, once more why you crashed?" She understood that Petey's fall and the hospital had become a catalyst for Sam.

He covered her hands with his. "This isn't the right time to talk about this."

"No time is *good,* Sam, not when you carry the past around your neck like an albatross. What was your *failure?* Did you take off in bad weather?" She waited, but he didn't reply. Gripping his fingers so tightly that her own fingers hurt, she held his gaze. "Tell me."

"All right! The weather was fine. It was a beautiful day." His face was haunted.

"Oh, I guess you forgot to make your preflight check? Forgot to file a flight plan?"

"No!" He was stretched as tight as a bowstring waiting for the arrow's release.

"You must have taken shortcuts on the maintenance of your plane, then."

"No!" His hands were holding on to hers as though he couldn't let her go.

"What did the investigators decide, Sam? Pilot error? You took an antihistamine before flying? Maybe you had a beer or two? Something like that?" Hannah stared him down, as tense as he. She lifted to her tiptoes so that she could see into his shaded eyes. "Did they find pilot error, Sam?"

His body sagged. "No."

"What did they conclude?" she whispered.

"Invisible metal fatigue."

She smoothed the wrinkles her fingers had made in his shirt. "An *accident*. Not your fault."

"I should have gotten them out of the plane when it crashed," he said. His voice carried the darkness of the grief he'd lived with for two years.

"How?"

He lifted his head.

"Your larynx was crushed. You were flung out of the airplane and were fifteen yards away with a broken pelvis, multiple fractures and head injuries. Arnie told me that much. Now, you tell me how you were supposed to get them out of the plane."

"I don't know. Somehow. I'm a man. I could have done *something*."

"*Only* a man? I'm surprised to hear you admit that. For a while I thought you believed you were God."

She wouldn't have believed Sam's face could go whiter, but it did. His voice was a low growl. "I think you better tell me what you mean by that."

Running her fingers through her hair, Hannah tried to sort out her chaotic thoughts. "You act as though you have God-like powers, Sam. All-seeing, all-knowing, all-powerful."

"I've never pretended that," he said, and his anger was a living presence between them. "That's a cruel thing to say, Hannah."

"Is it? Truly? Only someone with those powers could have prevented the crash. Could have saved your wife and infant son."

His mouth tightened, and he started to speak.

"You're not God. Don't punish yourself for being only a man."

"That's it. Enough." Turning to leave, he stumbled.

"Two more questions, Sam," Hannah said to his broad back, his dear back that had borne so much and wouldn't yield the load. "Indulge me, all right?"

His shoulders slumped, but he stopped. One hand braced himself against the tiled wall. His fingers were flexed, the knuckles white.

"What kind of God would exact the kind of retribution you have? You've denied yourself all of the earth's pleasures. Food, comfort. By sacrificing your own life, Sam, are you changing the past? Do you enjoy being a memorial?" Hannah let out the words in a rush.

Over his shoulder, Sam glared at her. From two feet away she could feel the heat of his anger. "Finished, Hannah?"

"Yes," she whispered, not moving an inch.

"Good." He limped out of her sight.

Hannah didn't expect to see him again.

But he was there, waiting, when she and Petey came out of the hospital.

"I'll take you home." Sam watched Hannah look up at him, her eyes start to shine and then dim. Her hair was every which way, her knees dusty with dried mud, and she was beautiful.

He was so furious with her he couldn't speak for a minute.

Trudging by her side, Petey looked up, and a smile creased his grimy square face. "Hey, Sam! I thought you didn't want to see me no more."

Sam couldn't look at Hannah. Her words still burned, and his anger was boiling inside, but his face softened as he smiled at Petey. "Now that's a dopey thing to think."

"You left."

"Yeah."

"But you're back. I knowed you would come home." Petey leaned against Sam with satisfaction. "And I got a harness. See?" He showed the padded straps and buckle to Sam.

Sam tested the buckle while managing not to look at Hannah.

"And it has to be tight so my bone will grow together where I splitted it."

"Good." Lifting Petey up, Sam hugged him and carried him to the Jeep with Hannah walking silently beside them.

Walking slowly so that he wouldn't stumble, missing his cane, Sam felt the tender weight of Hannah's son in his arms and gripped him tightly as he remembered the moment Petey tumbled off the fence and he couldn't run fast enough to save him.

Life was too uncertain to treat lightly.

He held Petey close to him and made his way to the Jeep.

At Hannah's house, he carried Petey upstairs, scowling Hannah into silence as she started to say she'd do it. All the way up the stairs, with Petey clinging like a barnacle to his neck, Sam heard Hannah's words in his ears.

"I'll get a washcloth," she said when they went into Petey's bedroom.

Propping Petey up on his pillows, Sam sank onto the edge of the bed. "Hurting now, aren't you?"

"Yeah. I was a doofus," Petey said. "I was a dumb bunny."

"Because you fell?" Sam heard Hannah turn on the water in the bathroom.

"Yeah." Tears slipped down Petey's cheeks. "I tried not to be."

"Some doofus." Sam grinned at him. "Fancy harness, all those good-looking nurses treating you like a king."

"And you came back. That's all I wanted, Sam. You back home. I was scared and worried when you was gone."

"Why?" Sam untied Petey's sneakers and pulled off his muddy socks.

"I was scared you was hurt."

"Me?" Sam tucked the socks inside the shoes. "Tough old me?" Glancing at the doorway, he saw Hannah hesitate and stay in the hall.

Petey's voice was a small whimper. "And I was worried you left 'cause I done something wrong and you didn't want me anymore. Like Daddy."

Sam froze. "Leave because of you?" Looking at Petey's brimming eyes, Sam knew Petey meant every word. "Now, why would I want to do a doofus thing like that?" He pulled the spread back.

"Daddy did."

Sam pleated the spread over and over in ever-smaller folds. "You really believe that, Petey? A smart kid like you?"

Petey nodded.

"I'm going to tell you a secret, okay?"

Nodding again, Petey watched him closely. "But I don't keep secrets from Mommy."

"Good. Listen, buddy. Grown-ups do real stupid things. They're dumb bunnies a lot more than they want to be, hear? Your daddy didn't leave because of *you.* I don't know for sure why he left, but you had nothing to do with it. You were not responsible." Sam heard Hannah's words echo in his mind.

"I was a bad boy. Daddies don't like bad boys." Petey still watched him.

"Of course they do. They love them. They just don't always know how to show their love."

"Daddy didn't want me for his boy no more." Petey's shoulders slumped and his chin trembled, but with a courage beyond his years, he held Sam's gaze.

"Damn it, kid." Sam lifted Petey right off the bed and sat him on his lap. The trusting warmth of Hannah's son in his arms broke his heart. "Listen, buddy." Sam cleared his throat. "Being your dad would make a man proud. You're loyal and brave. Funny. Nobody could want a better kid." Sam's fingers trembled against Petey's hair. "Hell, Petey, being your dad would be the biggest honor a man could hope for in life."

"Even with my foot?" Checking out everything, Petey wasn't yet convinced.

"Hey, look at my legs." Wishing, wishing he could take Petey's too-heavy burden on his own shoulders, wishing everything were different, Sam stuck out his legs.

Petey traced two scars and looked up. "Yeah." His smile was shaky. "You got two bum legs, but I love you, Sam." He wrapped his arms around Sam's neck.

Sam's throat was burning. He swallowed. "You're one hell of a kid, Petey Robert Randall. I love you, too." He cleared his throat. "Let's get you cleaned up, okay?"

"Yeah. And then Mommy will tell me a story."

Taking the cloth from Hannah, Sam wiped Petey's face and hands. "You'll take your medicine, your mommy will tell you a story and you're never going to blame yourself for the things grown-ups do, right?"

"Prob'ly not."

Sam rose carefully and faced Hannah.

"Thank you, Sam. Again." Standing in the doorway, she was distant and withdrawn.

He supported himself on the dresser at the foot of Petey's bed. "Goodbye, Hannah."

"I won't apologize for anything I said, Sam."

"Somehow I'm not surprised."

"I meant every single word." In front of him with her shoulders braced, her face stubborn and water dripping from her wet hands, Hannah wasn't about to give him any quarter.

She never had.

"Yeah. I know you meant what you said. But words don't change anything."

"They should." There was still a little anger bubbling under her words, too, and he heard the edge.

"Don't kid yourself, Hannah." He stared deep into her eyes. "Words may be powerful, but you can't change people with speeches." He knew he was being harsh, but she'd driven him to the wall and scored blood. He had to leave before he lashed out any more.

Passing her in the doorway, he felt her hair brush against his face, knew what he was walking out on, but he was still the same man inside.

And that man couldn't give Hannah and her son what they needed. He knew that, too.

Hannah walked to the front door with him, held it open, but she didn't say anything, just looked at him with an expression he couldn't decipher.

She'd obviously said everything she had to. And that had been plenty.

He had nothing to add. Not with all this anger hot and surging inside him.

An anger he was in no hurry to give up.

He'd come back to close up Arnie's house. He wasn't going to stay.

But he wouldn't leave this time without telling Petey first, though.

When he thought everything had been said, she added one more quiet statement. "You would have been a great hanging judge, Sam. You show no mercy, do you?"

She closed the door behind him, shutting him out.

Chapter Eleven

Hannah continued to take Petey with her when she worked at the preschool. She stayed away from her house during the day, making up errands, dragging Petey on every errand and shopping trip she could dream up. They spent a lot of time in the air-conditioned library. She didn't want to see Sam.

He'd been right. Words wouldn't change things.

Keeping Petey still for the first week was an unending task.

He slipped out to the yard every chance he could, and she heard him talking sometimes to Sam through the fence. She didn't say anything about it.

Fall would bring an end to the conversations. She still worried about Petey's attachment to Sam, but the damage had been done. She would just have to let time and new experiences ease Petey away.

Quiet lay uneasily on either side of the tall fence as the days grew hotter and summer dozed to its end.

School would start in two weeks. She welcomed it. Welcomed the respite it would give her. Once she was caught up in the whirl of papers and routine, she wouldn't think of Sam's face as she'd last seen it.

That uncompromising, self-condemning expression haunted her. He wouldn't forgive her for what she'd said to him.

Hannah thought about the way the half-drowned plants in Sam and Petey's garden had looked after the rain. She didn't think much of the garden had survived the hurricane's sideswipe. She was sorry for Petey. He'd counted on their harvest dinner.

One afternoon when she'd run out of made-up errands, she let Petey go over to Sam's to weed the garden. The happiness on his face when he came back broke her heart.

Love was a lot like those plants, she thought as she ran in her circle of never-ending errands, trying to escape from thinking about Sam and not able to.

The past was drowning Sam.

Whatever she felt for him would never survive the weight of what swept him along in its current.

She didn't want to give a name to the aching longings that woke her up and left her with purple circles under her eyes.

On Tuesday, she found an orange envelope addressed to Petey in her mailbox. Sam had sent him a birthday card.

Carl didn't. Not even a late card. Not even a call.

She wasn't surprised. And somehow, with Sam's card read over and over to him, Petey didn't seem to care, either.

He had changed over the summer, too.

Petey taped Sam's card carefully onto the refrigerator and told her she couldn't take it down even after his birthday had passed. The wise-cracking rabbit with the garish orange carrots stuck under a ridiculous purple hat grew smeared with Petey's fingerprints as he traced Sam's signature. Love, Sam.

"I love Sam and he loves me," he declared and looked at her with his head tilted to one side, studying her. "Do you love Sam?"

Hannah couldn't answer. Love was a two-way street, and Sam, well, Sam was stranded on some road of his own. "Petey, love is different for grownups." She flushed as, unbidden, a memory of Sam kissing her flashed and sparkled in her mind.

"Yeah. Kissing. I know about all that. But do you love Sam?" He was leaning on the kitchen table and waggling his rear end in time to the music from the radio.

"I—I can't answer that, Petey." But his question had made her face what she'd been avoiding, and she heard the catch in her throat and hoped Petey didn't. She handed him a piece of paper to write a thank-you note to Sam for the card.

Sam got the thank-you note. Scribbles, really. He held it between his fingers and then stuck it in the space between his mirror and its frame. He saw it first thing every morning.

He had walked out of Hannah's house and fed his anger through the hot days and nights. Had liked the boiling, hot rage running through him.

When Petey showed up from time to time, Sam felt the anger leave him and something sad take its place, but Petey wouldn't let him be sad for long and the time would pass in the blink of an eye.

But lying in bed, thinking of Hannah, watching the ceiling fan circle endlessly above him, Sam enjoyed pouring gasoline on his anger. There was wonderful satisfaction in the sheer ticked-offedness he felt. Sometimes he felt like storming over to her house and—

What?

Taking her shoulders and shaking her? Yelling at her? Stirring restlessly on top of his sheets while the air moved slowly over him, Sam knew that shaking Hannah was the last thing he'd do if he touched her.

Remembering the cloudy clinging of her hair, the silkiness of her skin, the soft slide of her mouth under his, he stirred again.

She'd had no right to say the things she had. She hadn't been there, lying in the dirt, trying to move with nothing working except his fingers, and they wouldn't drag him to the plane no matter how hard he'd tried.

If he'd gotten to the plane, it wouldn't have mattered. Like a lightning sizzle in the sky, the words streaked through his brain. *It was too late from the minute the plane hit the ground.* The crackle surging through him was as hair-raising as if lightning had struck him where he stood. *There was nothing he could have done to change anything.*

That night as he watched the fan circle around and around, the same way his thoughts circled and always returned to Hannah and Petey, Sam realized that he no longer heard Rachel's screaming in his mind. The sound that had haunted his nights had disappeared somewhere in his worries about Petey. The numbness he'd clung to in the past had vanished in the fierce emotions Hannah had called up, yielded to the anger and the craving his senses felt for her, yielded to the life Hannah and Petey had given back to him.

Sam could hear the beating of his heart, feel the warm air against his skin, the smooth sheet across his belly. He was alive. And he could finally forgive himself for surviving.

There was one instant when Rachel's face was blurry on the ceiling above him and he reached out to her, his fingers straining to her once more as they had for so long in his nightmares. But now, smiling joyously, she was holding Alex up to him so that he could see his chubby, blue-eyed boy. Rachel's eyes were bright with love. With forgiveness. With farewell.

She leaned toward him and air moved against his fingers as though she'd touched him. Even as he felt the gentle brush of air, her face, his son's, dimmed, leaving behind them peace.

Sam's hand dropped to his side, but the memory of Rachel's blue eyes filled with absolution stayed with him as he wiped away the tears sliding down his face.

* * *

The night of his birthday, Petey stayed a long time out-side chattering away in the dark. Hannah wanted to be out there with him, with Sam, but there was no future in it.

She stayed inside and turned the radio up.

Petey squirmed on the stump. "So why do you have to leave?"

"Because I've already made arrangements," came the dragon's voice.

"You could come live at my house."

"I don't think that would work." The dragon's voice was thoughtful.

Petey thought of the way his mommy had looked when he'd asked her if she loved Sam.

"I wish you would stay."

The red eye lifted. "I wish I could."

"I made a birthday wish."

"Oh?" The quiet rasp of the dragon's voice was hard to hear.

"It's the same wish I wished on the chicken bone."

"Terrific."

"Want to hear?" Petey wiggled again.

"You're not supposed to tell wishes."

"It's okay," Petey said. "Because I need you to help me one more time. I promise I'll never ask you again if you do this one last magic."

"I can't do magic, Petey." The dragon sent the smell of fire and smoke toward him.

Petey was worried he'd make the dragon mad, but he wasn't going to lose this chance. "I want Sam back. I love him."

There was no reply for a long time. Finally the dragon's voice came low to him, rough with regret. "It's not that easy."

"But Mommy loves him, too."

"What?" The raspy voice was harsh and the dragon stirred restlessly. "How do you know?"

"I asked her and I could tell, that's how. Me and Mommy need him, and I would very much like him for a daddy around all the time. You got to fix things. For my birthday wish. You're the only one who can do anything." Petey trailed off into silence as he waited. He brushed away a mosquito.

"I don't know."

"Try?"

"Maybe," growled the dragon, and Petey decided it was time to go. "Byethankyouverymuch," he sang out as he ran home.

In the kitchen, he patted the card Sam had given him and waited for the magic, drumming his feet impatiently against his chair.

Upstairs, going through Petey's clothes to see what she could salvage for the start of school and what she'd have to replace, Hannah heard the doorbell ring.

Dumping the stack on the bed, she pulled her T-shirt down over her bare tummy and headed downstairs. Looping up a strand of hair falling in her face, she jammed it into the coil on top of her head and opened the door.

"Sam?" Hannah clutched the door.

"Better close your mouth before you catch flies." The green tops of three puny carrots stuck out of one fist. In his other hand, he held out five summer squash, pale yellow and droopy.

"What are you doing?"

"It's like this, Hannah," he said as he propped himself against the open door, "I've come to invite you and Petey to a harvest dinner."

"What?" She shoved her hair away from her face.

"Sam!" Petey barreled down the hall.

"Hannah, listen to me, and listen carefully. I don't have a hell of a lot to offer you, but I can support you and Petey."

"Sam Dennehy, what in the world are you talking about?" She hoped, she wished, but she held on to the door as if her life depended on it, afraid to reach out to him.

"Me. You. Tiger over there. Us."

"Us?" she whispered. "Us?" Her hand slid down the door.

"Yeah." The shadows were gone from his clear hazel eyes and their shifting colors mesmerized her.

She couldn't have moved if the house were falling down around her, but she had to be sure. She gripped the edge of the door. "I don't need anybody to support me. I can take care of Petey."

"I know you can." Sam hesitated, and Hannah tried not to hope, tried not to want. "What about someone to warm your cold toes on cold nights, Hannah?" His voice was tentative.

"I can buy an electric blanket," she said, afraid to believe in miracles. "What do you want, Sam?" Her fingers were bonded to the door.

"You, Hannah. Petey. With me. Forever." The words were strong and filled with conviction.

"There's no such thing as forever, Sam," she said, her heart rising to her throat.

"I know." His chest rose and fell heavily. "Until death do us part, then, Hannah. Is that enough?"

"Not enough, Sam," she whispered past her tears, seeing heaven in front of her.

"I told you once to run, Hannah, but you wouldn't. Run now if you want to. I'm carrying a lot of baggage, for damned sure, and I wouldn't blame you if you take off like a bat out of hell, but if you do—" he reached out and brought her close, the feathery tops of the carrots tickling her neck "—I'm going to be right behind you. No matter how long it takes to catch up with you, bright eyes, I'm going to be right behind." His voice was husky, and he moved the carrot greens against her cheek.

"You'd be right behind me?" The trembling started in her hands and took over her whole body.

"Aw, Hannah." Sam gathered her in to him. "I can't let you and Petey get away from me. I couldn't stand it. I swear, bright eyes, I'll try not to fail you, but I'm not perfect, and there's a corner of my heart where Rachel and Alex will always be."

"Oh, Sam." Hannah rubbed her face against his shirt.

He made her look at him. "God knows, Hannah, you and Petey have all the rest of my heart. I love you so damned much it scares the hell out of me, but I can't let you go."

"Don't you know you're the missing half of myself, Sam Dennehy? If I run, it'll be real slow. I need you more than I ever thought I'd need anybody again except Petey," she murmured tearfully in his ear.

Sliding his carrot-filled hand to her hips, Sam pulled her tight against him. His kiss, urgent and fierce, sent them rocking back and forth against the door. The carrots and squash fell to the floor as he wrapped his arms around her.

Hannah felt Petey nudge between them as he clung very carefully to Sam's legs. She heard him mutter, "I told 'em he was real" just as Sam's mouth took hers again and sent thought and hearing somewhere out into space, leaving her only him, his heart, his arms holding her.

Petey watched as Hannah picked up the bunch of wildflowers. When she nodded, and she knew her smile was a little shaky, he took her elbow and walked with her across the yard to Sam, who was waiting under the oak tree where the smell of clover crushed by so many feet rose sweet and light in the air to her as she went to him.

She saw Petey's eyes grow huge, and he almost said something as they walked past the red-haired man with the gold earring. Hannah heard the "Way to go, cookie," and smiled at Louie, whose loopy grin sped her feet to Sam.

She waited while the minister asked, "Who gives this woman to this man?"

Petey turned her elbow loose and answered seriously and solemnly, "Me and my drag— I mean, I do, me, Petey Robert Randall gives my mommy to Sam. Forever."

Hannah leaned down and kissed him. "I love you to bits, sugar. I'm so proud of you."

And then she turned to Sam, and her eyes were shining as she looked at him.

Tall and strong, he towered over her, leaning only a bit on his new cane. His hair was sleeked back and smoothly trimmed and his eyes welcomed her home. She held out her shaking hand to him.

When he covered her fingers with his long ones and tucked her hand up close to him, she stepped next to him with her heart bursting with love.

Later, while a band played fiddle music, Petey flung himself in the grass off in the far corner of the garden and watched the fireflies land all around him.

Once he heard his mommy and Sam walk by.

Sam said, "You brought me back to life, Hannah. You and Petey are more important to me than you'll ever know, but I'm going to spend every waking moment trying to prove it."

"Shh, Sam, just kiss me."

Petey smiled. They were going to live here where the dragon lived. Sam had bought the house from Dr. Arnie.

Dozing in the warm evening air while the music swirled around him, Petey opened his eyes once.

Off in the distance he could see the faint, faraway glimmer of the dragon's red eye. It winked one final time at him and disappeared into the late-summer darkness.

*   *   *   *   *

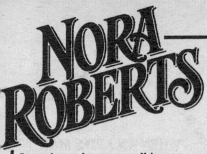

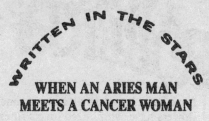

WRITTEN IN THE STARS

WHEN AN ARIES MAN
MEETS A CANCER WOMAN

Aggressive Aries businessman Alexander
Donaldson III did *not* appreciate being
wakened at dawn by a huge sheep outside his
bedroom window! But upon confronting its
owner—child psychologist Hannah
Martinof—Alex knew his love phobia was
instantly cured! Now, if only Hannah would
admit she wanted *him!* Carla Cassidy's
WHATEVER ALEX WANTS... is coming
this April—only from Silhouette Romance.
It's WRITTEN IN THE STARS!

Silhouette Special Edition

is pleased to present

A GOOD MAN WALKS IN
by Ginna Gray

The story of one strong woman's comeback
and the man who was there for her, Travis McCall,
the renegade cousin to those Blaine siblings,
from Ginna Gray's bestselling trio

FOOLS RUSH IN (#416)
WHERE ANGELS FEAR (#468)
ONCE IN A LIFETIME (#661)

Rebecca Quinn sought shelter at the hideaway on Rincon
Island. Finding Travis McCall—the object of all her childhood
crushes—holed up in the same house threatened to ruin the
respite she so desperately needed. Until their first kiss . . .
Then Travis set out to prove to his lovely Rebecca that man
can be good and love, sublime.

You'll want to be there when Rebecca's disillusionment turns
to joy.

A GOOD MAN WALKS IN #722

Available at your favorite retail outlet this February.

Silhouette Special Edition

salutes

MOMENTS OF GLORY

from Lindsay McKenna

In a country torn with conflict, in a time of bitter passions, these brave men and women wage a war against all odds... and a timeless battle for honor, for fleeting moments of glory, for the promise of enduring love.

February: RIDE THE TIGER (#721) Survivor Dany Villard is wise to the love-'em-and-leave-'em ways of war, but wounded hero Gib Ramsey swears she's captured his heart... forever.

March: ONE MAN'S WAR (#727) The war raging inside brash and bold Captain Pete Mallory threatens to destroy him, until Tess Ramsey's tender love guides him toward peace.

April: OFF LIMITS (#733) Soft-spoken Marine Jim McKenzie saved Alexandra Vance's life in Vietnam; now he needs her love to save his honor....

From the popular author of the bestselling title
DUNCAN'S BRIDE (Intimate Moments #349)
comes the

LINDA HOWARD

COLLECTION

Two exquisite collector's editions that contain four of
Linda Howard's early passionate love stories. To add
these special volumes to your own library, be sure
to look for:

VOLUME ONE: *Midnight Rainbow*
                  Diamond Bay
                  (Available in March)

VOLUME TWO: *Heartbreaker*
                  White Lies
                  (Available in April)

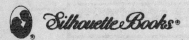
Silhouette Books®

SLH92